Kelly Bags & Crocodiles

The Diary of a Displaced Housewife

Linda Young

Published by L Young

© Copyright Linda Young, 2019

KELLY BAGS & CROCODILES
2nd Edition

ISBN 978-1-980-29007-0

Book formatted by www.bookformatting.co.uk

Contents

PART ONE
Gone With the Bailiffs

WEEK 1
Sun Damage

THURSDAY 10 JANUARY 2008

Arrived here safely, much to my surprise. Remained relatively calm on the journey, thanks to zero turbulence and my lovely GP prescribing a very generous dose of Valium. Even remained calm when almost ended up in the Bangkok Hilton for carrying a full bottle of contact lens solution. Hated the descent into Sydney as the runway is in the sea, but luckily the Captain was a much better driver than me and he managed to keep the nose right in the middle of the white line.

Stumbled off the 'plane and staggered through passport control to discover that all our luggage was still in Dubai. Devastated. Cried a bit. All very tired and ratty with each other anyway, so this was the last straw.

Our driver was waiting for us and he rang the husband's new boss to confirm that he'd collected "Allan and his women," then drove to Harrington Park. Girls and I gasped as we pulled up at the house – it's FABULOUS!

Staggered inside, went upstairs to have a bath and nearly fainted when I looked in the mirror. Staring back at me was a haggard old witch – make-up smudged, hair greasy, face spotty, hands, legs and feet swollen. I wore flight socks all the way from Manchester Airport until I walked through the front door here, but my legs still swelled up. My poorly coccyx was killing me after sitting down for so long, but I couldn't take pain-killers as they don't mix with tranquilisers. Had to make a choice between a state of terror or physical agony and decided to go with the agony – I have a high pain threshold!

Girls fell into bed and husband and I went shopping for essentials, bearing in mind the missing suitcases. Bought knickers, bras, t-shirts and toiletries, then went food shopping. Spent $300 in less than an hour.

Back to house after quick ride around the estate, then sent the husband out to buy pizza for dinner. We gobbled all the food then went to bed, hoping that our suitcases would turn up the next day. All the Manchester/Dubai transfer people had the same problem, so felt confident that they'd appear.

So, to sum up my first day in Aus – I was spotty and swollen, and had no clothes, make-up or contact lenses. Luckily though, we had one pair of GHD's in my hand luggage, so was hopeful this would see the teenagers through the crisis until the other two pairs arrived. Went to bed exhausted and worried – this was supposed to be a better life than my old one, but so far it was proving stressful and expensive.

FRIDAY 11 JANUARY

Slept really well on first night here, despite being on a blow-up mattress. Woken very early though, by the parrots screeching outside. Went back to sleep and was woken up by husband's customer phoning to place an order – surely a good omen? Had a shower and put on what little make-up I had with me (luckily, I had bought a very nice MAC lipgloss trio in Duty Free) and went downstairs in glasses as contact lenses were in the missing suitcase. Had left hair to dry naturally as we only have one hairdryer between three of us.

Walked into kitchen and everyone fell about laughing. They were embarrassed to be seen with me and wanted to leave me at home while they went out. Had to endure ridicule all day over my appearance. To make matters worse, both girls appeared looking like supermodels, despite the difficult circumstances and lack of beauty aids, and wanted to know why I couldn't pull off the same stunt! Patiently explained that it had something to do with there being thirty years age difference between us, and me being on the wrong side of 40.

When they finally stopped laughing, we went to Eastern Creek Quarantine Station to pay Jasper Conran's kennel fees ($800!) There was another English family in Reception, also settling their bill for a dog named Jasper and their luggage had also gone astray – but they had been waiting more than a week for it to turn up. Husband thinks that with our luck, we'll turn up to collect Mr Conran on Sunday and we'll be given some old mongrel while our little pedigree darling will have been given to the wrong family!

Had exciting afternoon in Ikea at Homebush. Was like being newly-married all over again. Bought desk and bookcase for study, mixing bowls, pans, crockery etc. for kitchen, throws and cushions for lounge and towels and mats for bathroom. Was really tired when we got back in the truck – am very jet-lagged and my energy disappears by 2.00pm.

Had been home from Ikea just two minutes when doorbell rang – it was a courier with two of our suitcases; mine and Lulu's. Was so relieved I could have kissed him (believe me, he would have recoiled in horror). He'd just left when we had a call from the airline to say the other two cases were on their way.

Went to Harrington Plaza and bought cooked chicken, salad and garlic bread and had a very nice (and healthy) dinner. Was in my pyjamas eating dinner when the doorbell rang once more. Thought it was the courier again, but it was our first visitor. Luckily the husband answered the door, not me! It was a family whom the school have put in touch with us. They have 2 girls similar ages to Annie and Lulu, and they came to invite us to a BBQ on Sunday evening. I rang the mum (Rebecca) after dinner to accept, and she said to tell girls to bring "swimmers" as they have a pool. Girls not keen on this. We'll see how it goes.

Just after they'd left, the doorbell rang again and this time it WAS the courier, so now we have all our cases back. We are SO relieved. Can't wait to have another bath and get ready properly.

Girls are relieved to have their own GHDs back again. They both seem to be okay, although they're sceptical about making new friends and do not have very high expectations. I just keep telling them they have to concentrate on their schoolwork and get good grades.

The husband is like a dog with twenty tails and walks around saying BEAUUUUUTIFUL all the time. It's very annoying. He says he's like this because he has no stress over here. Just wait until the teenagers start moaning – that will stress him out.

So far it all feels like being on holiday, and living in this massive house is very exciting. The hallway is like something from Gone With the Wind. Sadly, my waist does not resemble Scarlett's waist, but I am back on my diet now and we are all going to circuit the lake together every night. Desperately need to get my waistline in co-ordination with the glamorous surroundings! By the way, at Dubai airport I had to put my belt through the scanner and when I put it back on, it seemed a bit tight. I looked around and saw a skinny old Indian man wrapping my very generous belt around him about five times, and realised we'd got a bit mixed up!

SATURDAY 12 JANUARY

Went to buy a washing machine and some bedroom furniture. Luckily found suitable items at first two places we tried – am too jet-lagged to shop. Washing machine arriving Monday morning and new bed will be here on Tuesday – cannot last any longer on the blow-up mattress.

To my dismay have discovered a MAJOR problem already. Have only been in Sydney for three days and have realised that I definitely need Botox. The bright sunshine is making me squint, and I'm developing a deep furrow on my brow which rivals that of Wallis Simpson! Think I need to get some HUGE sunglasses in the style of Victoria Beckham (now I'm back to thinking about tiny waists again!)

SUNDAY 13 JANUARY

All up very early to go and fetch Jasper Conran from the Quarantine Station. Arrived far too early and had to queue up outside the electric gate. Eventually went in to reception and had our documents checked, then a kennel girl instructed us to follow her. She led us over to the back of a trailer and pulled aside the curtain – inside were about ten animal crates. Jasper's was the first little face I spotted and the poor little boy looked absolutely petrified. We carried his box over to our truck and lifted him out. He cried when he saw me - he'd obviously thought he was back in the box for another long journey. He was very quiet for most of the day, and he follows me absolutely everywhere – even into the loo!

Sadly, we had to leave him in his new cage (which is very spacious, and we left a fan on him) while we went to the BBQ. We walked round to the house – very big with a huge garden and large swimming pool. The family were very friendly and very kind to us. We had steak and salad and potatoes in cheese sauce – it was raining heavily but still very hot and we ate at a massive table under a huge gazebo, which easily held all eight of us. We stayed about five hours and had a really nice time.

Went to bed exhausted tonight, only for Jasper Conran to have me up about five times. He needed lots of 'toilet breaks' as he's drinking so much in this heat.

WEEK 2
Puff Mummy

<u>TUESDAY 15 JANUARY</u>

Stayed in bed most of yesterday and my jet-lag is much better now, but I look just awful – bags under my eyes, dry skin, puffy face. Hope I adjust to this heat very soon as I can't bear looking like this – thank goodness I don't know anyone yet.

Bed was delivered today – hallelujah!

<u>WEDNESDAY 16 JANUARY</u>

Went shopping this afternoon, alone, to Macarthur Square shopping Mall at Campbelltown. Husband dropped me off at 1.30pm and collected me again at 4.30pm, but sadly I got lost and couldn't find my way back to where he dropped me off! I was almost in tears, which made the cruel teenagers laugh their socks off when I told them. Had to ask at Information Desk and finally found where I needed to be. Bought some magazines in Borders and smuggled them into the house (husband disapproves of my magazine habit).

Read a feature in Instyle on different Australian holiday destinations, and one of them was Byron Bay. Am now trying to get the girls into the Byron Bay beach look, which is a lovely long printed cotton dress worn with a denim waistcoat – very cool. However, it doesn't appear as if they'll be parted from their jeans and Converse any time soon!

At dinner-time tonight, we all sat around and waited for the husband to feed us. Really must get out of this habit. Because he lived here for two months before us, we think of it as being his house and ourselves as his guests, so we all wait around for him to make the meal. It's worked every night so far, but he's getting fed-up with it (especially since he's actually been working every day) so I think I'll have to cook tomorrow. Was nice to sit down at our new table (very chic, circular black glass top) and actually eat and chat together – at only 6.00pm. This was unheard of back home as he was never there before 7.30pm at the earliest.

THURSDAY 17 JANUARY

Have discovered there is a Weight Watchers meeting held at Harrington Park. Doubt I will go though, as feel sure I must be internationally blacklisted and branded a quitter. Was reading local paper (Camden Advertiser) when I came across a column entitled "Camden Weekly Fatstock Report." Thought it must be something to do with dieting, and worried that shameful weigh-in results were printed for all to see, but when I read further it turned out to be the cattle prices!

Weather seems to be very varied here and we had a much cooler day today, thank goodness. Annie went to work with her dad today. He was round and about building sites in Sydney and they had a good day together.

Lulu stayed here with me. She went back to bed after they left and slept until 1.00pm. She was tired after staying up all night to communicate with friends back home, who were all off school under the guise of coughs, colds, tummy upsets and "feeling poorly." I suspect there will be a lot of people sneaking off school when they realise they can stay home and MSN with Lulu all day.

Spent this morning organising my clothes and sorting the laundry. Realised that I now have a whole new vocabulary in my life – dressing room, en-suite, rumpus room, balcony, utility room, linen cupboard, guest room and downstairs loo (known as the Powder Room over here). Am trying not to get carried away though, as we might be out of here by the end of May.

Had a ride out tonight towards the Razorback Mountains. Didn't go too far as not enough time, but was a very interesting drive out – it all looks very 'American,' like a Western!

Meeting scheduled at school for tomorrow afternoon, so girls will get a feel of what they're in for.

Doorbell rang late tonight and it was Rebecca. She was out walking their Doberman and had called to ask if girls wanted to go to the library with her girls tomorrow. Had to say no as it clashes with school meeting. She also mentioned she's arranging a trip to the movies and would like to invite Annie and Lulu. She's very kind to go to such trouble for us.

FRIDAY 18 JANUARY

School meeting went very well. The Registrar was very helpful and spent a lot of time going over everything and showing us around the school. Hope girls will be happy there. Annie asked quite a few questions, but Lulu was very quiet. Neither of them are very pleased about having to go to school camp on the first week back after the holiday. On 29 January they go away for 3 nights doing 'adventure' stuff such as bushwalking, canoeing, abseiling etc. They were a bit alarmed to see from the itinerary that the first session deals with emergency first aid, covering issues such as snake and spider bites! I would prefer to keep them at home and send them to school the week after camp, but I don't think that would be in their best interests. They just need to dive straight in and get on with meeting people. They will be fine. It will be me who has the hard time, worrying about them!

Weather was cool again today, and it rained all afternoon. Such a welcome change. When I put my make-up on after my shower, the make-up has disappeared before I've finished drying my hair! Even my Bobbi Brown eye-liner, which stays put all day at home, wears off here in no time. Thankfully though, I've solved one of my problems – I found some John Frieda frizz-ease in the supermarket, so am hopeful of getting my hair back to normal.

The big news over here is that Nicole (Kidman) is pregnant –

hope we get invited to the christening. I quite fancy Keith; he's like a rougher, cooler, sexier version of Tom Cruise. Pity about his name though. 'Keith' and 'cool' don't really go together.

SATURDAY 19 JANUARY

Nightmare day today. Had to go and buy all the equipment that girls need for the school camp. List was a mile long and cost a fortune. Had HUGE row in BigW changing room as they refused to wear any of the shorts I'd picked out. Naughty girls just kept laughing at each other and refusing to have anything. They've also got to take a wide-brimmed sunhat and that brought on absolute hysteria. Couldn't find half the gear they needed. Only managed to buy sunblock and mosquito repellent - no water bottles, cutlery, sleeping bags etc. Need to ring school again and clarify some of the items, eg socks - long or short? Sleeping bag - indoor or outdoor? And what on earth is a 'daypack?' Is all a nightmare. Wish I'd made an excuse now and said they would start school the week after camp. Too late now. Have to go shopping again tomorrow and try to buy the rest of the list.

Have been very jittery about snakes today. Was reading the Camden Advertiser again and there was an article called, "Defeat the Snakes by Clearing Up." It says you must keep your grass short so there's nowhere for them to hide. Now need to organise someone to come and mow the lawns. The next door neighbour has cut it for us quite a few times, but we need to get properly organised. Will sort it out on Monday.

Have realised that I'm missing my music. Will be pleased when girls are at school and Jasper Conran and I can play Bruce, Bryan and Elvis as loud as we want (that's Springsteen, Adams, Presley and Costello). Bruce, Elvis (Presley) and Aerosmith kept me going on the final leg of the flight over here. (Also listened to Kenny Rogers, but don't tell anyone). Will be so glad when my cds finally arrive.

Had very sad email from sister tonight. She's missing me, but is also sad because her eldest son is 18 next week and she feels very old! I too feel very old, and also very ugly. Yes, I still look pretty bad at the moment. Bought some jogging pants in BigW and will begin fitness regime on Monday.

SUNDAY 20 JANUARY

Puffy face appears to be receding, thank goodness.

WEEK 3
The Happy Housewife

MONDAY 21 JANUARY

Went jogging this morning – well, technically it was more of a power walk, but the main thing is that I did actually go. Enjoyed a little snooze afterwards, but feel sure that's allowed. Ate wholewheaty cereal and skimmed milk for breakfast. Unfortunately, I had a KFC for lunch, but promise to try harder tomorrow.

Decided to go shopping. I've been having John Lewis withdrawal symptoms so decided to cheer self up with a little shopping session. Took girls to Macarthur Square, drew out $200 and hit the arcades.

Luckily, in first 5 minutes we found a department store called "David Jones." Bought make-up, stationery, eye-lash curlers, fake-tan lotion and a massive black sunhat. Girls were not very amused by my sunhat purchase, but tough. We went to Gloria Jean's Coffee Shop for ice-cream smoothies (forgot I was on a diet) and when we'd finished, they left the carrier bag with my hat in it underneath the table. 20 minutes elapsed before I realised what had happened and sent them back for it. Luckily, a kind shopper had handed it to the waitress. Naughty girls swear they didn't do it on purpose, but I don't believe them. To punish them I'm going to wear my hat every morning when I walk them to the school bus stop. That'll teach them.

Husband picked us up from the mall after work and on way home we called at BigW to buy an iron, ironing board and clothes airers. Will have to stay in tomorrow and get up-to-date with the laundry.

On one of my last shopping trips before I left for Sydney, I bought a book in Waterstones called "The Happy Housewife" by Darla Shine (it's American). It's all about finding pleasure in running an efficient home and making a 'career' out of being a good housewife. She tells you to put a 'jaunty' bow in your hair before your husband gets home, and to wear a hat if you're having a bad hair day (not sure about the bow, but I'm all set on the hat front). Despite all the 'submissive little woman' nonsense, the main message is that we should be content with what we've got and not spend our lives shopping for items that we don't really need.

Have decided that Darla is right, so am not going to go to the mall anymore. Am going to concentrate on running the house and looking after husband, children and dog. Will not buy any more ready-made lasagnes or cooked chickens, but will power-walk to Harrington Plaza every day and buy fresh food for the evening meal. Have told the husband I need a budget of $250 per week, and hopefully this will enable me to have some money left over for any emergency purchases such as Benefit make-up or Clarins beauty serums. Will begin tomorrow.

TUESDAY 22 JANUARY

Such a good day here today. Looked up Darla Shine on the internet this morning and was amazed to see that she has a HUGE following and has her own 'club' on the internet – The Happy Housewives Club! Didn't join (am not dedicated enough yet) but was very amusing.

Took Jasper Conran out very early this morning, before the heat became too much to bear. He can't go very far before he lies down on the pavement in the manner of a dying dog, so we only went round two blocks and then back home.

Anyway, back to the Happy Housewife routine. Washed all the duvet covers today, and also cleaned all the bathrooms (living in a huge house is not so amusing when you have to clean it yourself!)

Was about to set off on my walk to the Plaza to buy fresh, healthy food for dinner when I just sat down on my bed to tickle Jasper's tummy for 5 mins and the next thing I knew it was 6.00pm and the husband was home from work. No shirts ironed and no meal prepared. No food in the fridge to even prepare. Darla would be very disappointed with me. Had to send family out to buy dinner while I finished my nap. They bought a quiche, garlic bread and salad, which was all very nice. Annie served it all and tidied up afterwards, which was even nicer. Must try harder tomorrow.

Didn't mention to husband, but did manage to find time to read Australian Vogue. Magazines are not really in my budget any more, but I don't think Darla would mind as am only LOOKING at the gorgeous, aspirational items, rather than planning to actually buy them. Will definitely try harder tomorrow.

WEDNESDAY 23 JANUARY

I want a pair of Ray-Bans. I NEED a pair of Ray-Bans. Apparently, the Wayfarers are back in fashion. I will be doing the husband a favour by buying a pair because my Wallis Simpson furrowed brow is getting worse every day, and soon I will definitely need Botox. As we all know, Botox has to be repeated every 8-9 months and costs hundreds of dollars per shot. If you reckon up the cost of that over the next 30 or 40 years, a pair of Wayfarers would be an absolute bargain – I'm saving him thousands! He should be BEGGING me to let him buy me a pair. Will see what he says when I put it to him. Will choose moment very carefully.

Have been a very good housewife today. Was jolted into action when Annie revealed to me that her father had a moan to her yesterday that he was fed-up with me acting as if I'm on holiday, and he'll be pleased when I "get my finger out and get on with some housework," ie making dinner every night and doing some washing and ironing, most crucially his work shirts. Decided I'd pushed my luck for long enough and finally did the laundry. By the time he returned from work, ALL his work shirts were hanging in his side of the dressing room, neatly washed and ironed. Clean pants and socks were in his chest of drawers, and I'd tidied away all my bits of paper that were lying around his desk. (I keep forgetting that the study is for him to actually use for proper work, rather than for me and the girls to mess around on the computer!)

After laundry duties, Annie and I walked down to the Plaza (this is really just a posh name for the shopping precinct) to buy dinner. On the way we discovered an absolutely fabulous house for sale. It's brand-new and not quite finished yet. We had a peep though the window and the kitchen was absolutely out of this world. The front door has video entry and doesn't even need a key – you just swipe your fingerprint! We went to the builder's office which is in the Business Suite at the Plaza, but the office manager knew nothing about this house – according to her records this plot was still empty! She was supposed to email me when the boss returned but has not done so yet. Doesn't sound hopeful. Probably too expensive for us. There are lots of houses for sale on the estate now, and new For Sale signs are going up every day. Interest rates have risen in Australia and many people are finding themselves with negative equity. If we could just sell the house back home, we could probably pick up a real bargain here. (Hope that doesn't sound callous – I do feel sorry for the people who are stuck with negative equity, but still, a bargain sounds good).

Annie and I had lunch at the Plaza – at Michel's Patisserie. Sadly, once again I forgot that I was dieting and ate a delicious vanilla slice after a yummy cheese croissant! Also keep forgetting to take my thyroid tablets – really must get into a routine. Actually, am not too worried about mistakenly eating a vanilla slice because I have realised that we are all eating far, far less than we used to do at home. For dinner today we had chicken (again), salad, quiche and garlic bread. Also, watermelon for starters. The amount on our plates is miniscule compared to what we ate before. I don't know if it's the heat that makes us eat less, or the novelty of our new life, but we just eat so much less. We have no bathroom scales here so for the first time in more than 20 years I'm not able to get weighed every day. Am just waiting for my clothes to get loose on me and then I'll know I'm losing weight. Must remember not to eat any

16

more vanilla slices or ice-cream smoothies. Will try harder tomorrow.

After dinner tonight, we persuaded the husband to take us out for a drive. We drove through Camden, Narellan and Campbelltown, then out into the countryside. The town centres are really nice. This area is an old colonial township and some of the buildings look like they're out of a western! The bank in Camden is brilliant and so is the newspaper building in Campbelltown. Our local sweetshop is called the Candy Cane Cottage and looks like something out of Hansel & Gretel.

I ought to go to bed now because I will need all my strength for tomorrow's ordeal – we're going into school at 8.00am for our appointment with the Uniform Fitting lady. Am not going to get involved with this – will just hand girls over to the relevant person and let her deal with them. Suspect there will be tears and tantrums.

THURSDAY 24 JANUARY

Won't be asking for any Ray-Bans – the husband has just written a cheque for almost $15,000 to cover school fees and uniforms! That only covers Annie's school fees – we're paying Lulu's fees over the next 11 months. We bought some of the uniform out of the 'clothing pool' (second-hand) as they were almost new and girls didn't object (too loudly). Bought both blazers new though, and they look very smart. Simply handed girls over to uniform ladies and left them to it while we went to Admin to sort out the fees.

When we'd finished at school, we went to BigW (yet again) to buy the last of the items for camp – cheap trainers (much to Lulu's dismay) and sand shoes. Think that's now everything covered. Can't believe it's cost so much money to send my children off into mortal danger! School should be paying me for allowing them to go (similar situation to husband and the Ray-Bans!)

The ladies in the school uniform shop were very kind. One lovely lady insisted on giving me her mobile number and told me to 'phone her if there was anything at all I needed help with. Am finding that all Australians are very caring. Feel sure there are probably exceptions somewhere, but luckily we haven't met them yet. People offer help without you having to ask for it, and are very concerned that we are are settled and happy. I can't imagine there's any area of Australia where the people are kinder than those of the Macarthur region.

Am hoping the husband is in a good mood when he gets home. Am going to suggest that we book a table at a seafood restaurant in Campbelltown one night next week when the girls are away at camp. Despite the lack of funds, I think we need a treat and a romantic night out by ourselves. A flyer advertising "El Gusto's" arrived in the post last week and I carefully stashed it away. On their lobster nights, you can get a whole lobster for $33.90 and can choose from garlic butter, mornay or napoletana sauces.

FRIDAY 25 JANUARY

Woke up in contemplative mood. Feel I need an incentive to keep me focused on my diet. Been out power-walking again this morning, and had wheaty flakes for breakfast, but I feel I need some gorgeous, silky, glittery, floaty, trinkety-type garment hanging in my wardrobe for me to fondle and admire every day. It will keep me on-track with my fitness regime and will be much, much cheaper than a personal trainer – will actually be saving the household quite a lot of money when you think about it. Have seen some gorgeous things on the internet, particularly love the Liz Hurley kaftan – which was approved by the teenagers, but have been told that under no circumstances will they allow me to wear white trousers! Am not bothered as would look very bad in them anyway, as do not possess Liz Hurley's concave stomach. Am going to the mall, but only to look. Don't tell Darla. Definitely don't tell the husband.

Went to Camden instead of mall. Camden is brilliant, I love it. Parts of it remind me of a wild west town. Bet it was brilliant being a pioneer in the olden days of Australia – think I would have been very brave and stoic. Would have been very good at making a living from the harsh, barren land, toiling in the fields beside a ruggedly handsome husband. Maybe it would have cured my fear of snakes, spiders and now kangaroos.

Drove out to Cronulla tonight and ate a delicious meal at a pavement café, under huge white umbrellas. Jasper Conran shared the husband's lamb salad, girls had pizza and I had pasta. Afterwards, we walked along the seafront and watched the surfers. I cannot get my head around why anyone would want to be in the sea in a country where there are sharks – all completely beyond my comprehension. Anyway, we set off back home at 8.00pm and for some unknown reason the SatNav directed us home a different way. We ended up on a very lonely stretch of highway where there were signs warning of kangaroos on the road. The husband had already been warned by his boss that if you're going to collide with a kangaroo, you have to make sure you hit it when it's landed on the ground, not when it's in mid-air, otherwise it comes through the windscreen and you're dead because some of them can weigh around 90kg. As it was now dusk (and they come out at night) I sat in terror, avidly watching the roadsides for any sign of them. Made the husband turn off the cd (much to his annoyance) so we could concentrate properly. Was very relieved when we came off the kangaroo road and were back on the outskirts of Liverpool. In future, the husband will have to programme the SatNav to avoid both tunnels AND kangaroos. Wonder what new swear words he will invent for that scenario!

SATURDAY 26 JANUARY

Sunhats are the bane of my life. It is COMPULSORY for girls to take a wide-brimmed sunhat to camp, but they are refusing to address the subject with any seriousness. Lulu has stated that the only type of hat she will countenance is a black trilby. As I refused to buy her one, she now won't discuss the subject at all. Annie does at least try hats on but refuses to make a decision about which one to buy, so we always return empty-handed.

Even my lovely new sunhat has turned out to be a deep disappointment – it makes me look fatter than ever. Does not at all project the image I was aiming for. Might have to investigate the straw stetsons worn by the Chelsea-tractor-driving yummy mummies on their holidays in the Caribbean. Only problem with that is they buy them from the Melissa Odabash Boutique in London – not the K-Mart in Campbelltown!

To add to my troubles, have just been on the Liz Hurley beachwear website. The opening photo of her is absolutely stunning and made me realise that my stomach is about 10 times the size of hers. Even her gorgeous Starfish blue kaftan will not make me look glam. Think I need surgery, but I have a deep-rooted fear of anaesthetic – and the husband has a deep-rooted fear of the cost of plastic surgery!

On a more serious note, the Starfish blue kaftan is absolutely gorgeous. It comes in long or short, and you can get a beach bag, mini beach bag and a sunhat to match. The kaftan is made from silk and the sunhat and bags are made from velvety, Italian cotton towelling. Feel sure they're easily worth their (slightly steep) pricetags. What price a wife's happiness, peace-of-mind and self-esteem?

PS: Was Australia Day today – BBQ parties all along the street, until the early hours. Think we're the only family in the country not celebrating!

SUNDAY 27 JANUARY

Another brilliant Sunday. Husband went to the supermarket and then prepared and packed a picnic while girls and I had showers, did hair and make-up etc. Drove to Shellharbour. Ate picnic in the car as was far too hot to eat outside without umbrellas, then got out for a walk. The resort was lovely – padding pool and swimming pool right next to the sea, but obviously safe from sharks etc. Was dying to get into the pool but hadn't brought any 'swimmers' (getting into the local lingo) so we walked up the hill and browsed the trendy little boutiques instead.

Against my better judgement, Lulu came out of the first boutique wearing a chocolate brown, suede trilby! Cost the husband

20

$20, but at least it will go to camp with her. She will have to wear her desert scarf as well though, because the brim is definitely not the stipulated regulation size. Annie ended up buying a hat she doesn't actually like, just because it was from a cool surf shop. I wanted her to get a turquoise straw stetson which really suited her, but no chance. Made them wear the hats straight away, despite protests. Husband also wore his hat today, which mortified the teenagers, but he sensibly declared he is only interested in protecting his (rapidly) balding head, not what he looks like! Didn't wear my hat, which is a bad example, I know, but family would have disowned me. Will have to go shopping again and resolve the sunhat crisis once and for all.

During long cool bath tonight, had a very stern word with myself about all this desiring of silken kaftans and cotton beach bags etc. Don't know where it all came from, especially after my resolutions about being a good housewife, as advocated by the sensible Darla Shine. Actually, I DO know where it all came from – those glamorous magazines. Have spent far too much time recently, gazing at page after page of lovely things. This must be why the husband disapproves of them so vehemently – it's not just the money they cost, it's that they make me restless and dissatisfied. So, no more. Have got to give up glossy magazines, along with Diet Coke. Will go cold turkey from midnight tonight. (Must just say though, I would REALLY like a new digital camera, preferably a Nikon).

Am going now – need to iron girls' clothes for camp and sew on name tapes (luckily, I brought name tapes with me). Have to say, although I am absolutely dreading sending them off tomorrow, I think I need the emotional rest from all the attitude they're giving me. They keep quoting my words back at me, so if I complain about anything at all they both chant, "Just get on with it; it will be character building." It is all very wearing. Have been looking forward to putting my feet up with a magazine while they're away, and drinking gallons of diet coke, but will obviously have to take a raincheck on that now. Will go jogging twice a day instead.

WEEK 4
Puppy Love

MONDAY 28 JANUARY

Bought the Camden Advertiser and tried to check out the Camden Weekly Fatstock Report but could not find it this week. Wanted to see if the Good Bobbies and Light Vealers had held their price.

Lulu is in a sulk because she has no alarm clock for camp. I explained that she shouldn't worry because the camp leaders will wake everybody up. She replied that she wanted to be up before everyone else so that she would have time to "do her hair." I don't think she realises that in the bush there will be nothing to "do" it with, except for a hairbrush. She appears to have just realised that she won't be able to take the straighteners. Or her black eye-liner. Or her red nail varnish. She also wanted to take her Darren Shan book (a teenage series about vampires). Had to put my foot down and say that taking a vampire book away on an Anglican church school camp, where the first item on the list of requirements is a bible, was NOT a good idea!

TUESDAY 29 JANUARY

My poor babies have gone to camp. I am worried sick and feel like the worst mother on earth for making them go. Wish I'd come up with an excuse now. If they just come back safely, I promise never to drink diet coke again. Ever. Have realised something terrifying. On the list of essentials for camp, two of the items were a long-sleeved shirt and long trousers. I naively thought this would be for some kind of churchy, bible-reading session, so the children looked smart instead of wearing shorts and t-shirts. I now know better. It was for when they go caving – so that the snakes and spiders can't run up their arms and legs. I feel sick.

Both girls looked very shaky this morning. Annie was trying to be stoical about it all. She was introduced to her head of year and to the camp leader. They took her off to the courtyard to join all the other year 10s. We saw her return and get on the bus, but she was walking by herself and I felt totally devastated. Wanted to run and bring her back to the car.

Lulu couldn't sleep last night, and looked very, very nervous this morning. She looked on the verge of tears when we left her. I was dismayed to realise that she was wearing her Converse instead of sensible new walking trainers, and also that she was wearing black eye-liner and mascara! She assured me that the sensible walking trainers were in her bag (along with the ridiculous trilby). She was introduced to her head of year and then whisked away to join the others. We waited to see her bus depart too, but view was blocked by other cars so didn't actually see her get on the bus.

In order to take my mind off my worries about the poor little girls, husband took me to the pub and insisted I had a couple of glasses of dry Strongbow (was delicious). My first drop of alcohol since New Year's Eve. We went to a brilliant pub in Camden, called The Crown. It's really modern inside, but very traditional outside. After the cider we sat outside 'Seagulls' café and ate fish and chips. Amused ourselves by feeding chips to the teeny tiny little sparrows. Strangely, I seem to have lost my fear of bird flu, despite being much nearer to the epi-centre. Although I did stumble across a very frightening website on the subject the other day. Best not to think about it. We also called at the Cheesecake Shop on the way home, as we needed to take our minds off our poor imperilled children by indulging in a spot of comfort eating. Felt very guilty after eating choc-chip cheesecake, as it's Annie's favourite. Will buy a whole one for them to eat when they get home on Friday.

Jasper Conran has been very, very naughty for the last two days.

When we got home from our evening drive last night, next door's cat was on our lawn and Jasper went absolutely berserk. He was screaming and crying and trying to chase it. When we got inside the house, he was still full of devilment and would not settle down. From the study window you can see the yard at the side of the house next door, where they hang out their laundry. On the washing line the neighbours have hung out a mop-head and it looks like it's resting on the top of our fence. Jasper obviously thinks this is another cat, so he keeps LAUNCHING himself into the window, sending the blinds flying and breaking the little plastic chain attached to the bottom. He is driving me insane. After half-an hour of battering himself against the window last night, he disappeared upstairs. Lulu came down 10 minutes later to inform me that he'd done a massive poo on the landing. I was furious with him. I hope he gets over this obsession with the mop very quickly. Allan took him outside to introduce him to it, in the hope that he'd realise it wasn't a cat. He lifted him right up so that he could sniff it, but it made him worse. He appears to be in love!

WEDNESDAY 30 JANUARY

Couldn't sleep last night, was too worried about girls, so am very, very weary today. Also very weepy. It's absolutely boiling hot here and feel worried sick about girls being out in this heat. Am going out to Coles to buy a heart-shaped muffin tin (Lulu wanted to buy one last week) to bake some buns for their return. Jasper is still driving me mad over the mop, think he is in love with it. Wish it was Friday.

Am feeling a bit better this evening – partly due to husband insisting he take me out for more Strongbow, but mainly due to Lulu's head of year ringing to let us know that she was ok. We were in the truck, en-route for Strongbow, when the carphone rang on loudspeaker. When the teacher introduced herself I nearly fainted with worry, and the husband also went a bit pale, as we thought there might be a problem. But she's fine, apparently, and she's made some friends. She's got a bit of sunburn on her nose (that stupid trilby), but apart from that she's had no problems. I wanted to ask which activities they'd done so far, so that I would know if the caving was over and done with, but I didn't really get the chance. It was very kind of her to ring – she said that as a mother herself, she knew we would be worried. Apparently, all the children were in the pool as she was speaking to us, so at least Lulu will be cooling off and relaxing. Hope she likes the food. Wish there was news of Annie.

THURSDAY 31 JANUARY

DING DONG THE MOP HAS GONE! We might get some peace and quiet now, without the mad dog head-butting the window. Saw the neighbour swabbing the poolside last night, and this morning the mop has been left to dry in a new spot. Jasper very quiet now, keeps gazing sadly out of the window – think he's pining for his lost love!

Wish I could report that the resident witch has also gone, but sadly not. Looked in mirror this morning – AFTER doing hair and make-up – and she was back again (not sure that she ever went very far). My hair is WILD. What am I going to do? Daren't straighten hair too much as afraid it might fall out if it gets any drier. Deep down I think I know the answer. Actually, I KNOW that I know the answer – I need to wear a hat constantly to protect hair from the damaging sunshine. My problems just keep going round and round in a circle, yet never get resolved. I look like Endora from Bewitched, and I SO want to be Samantha. Samantha was a good housewife who always had Tabitha in bed by 6.00pm and a cocktail ready for Darrin when he arrived home from work. Suspect she wouldn't look twice at a glass of Strongbow.

On way home from pub last night, husband INSISTED that we stop at the garage to buy me a magazine and some diet coke. He thought it might help take my mind off the poor camping children. I bought Harpers Bazaar Australia and I have to say that it DID help for a few hours. Harpers is fabulous, but am finding Australian magazines very confusing – the January, February mags are all featuring swimwear (very depressing when you've got my stomach) and gorgeous summer clothes, when my head keeps telling me they should be showing winter stuff. Will just have to keep on buying them until I become acclimatised.

Fabulous advert in Harpers for "Coach" the fashion brand, which showed a (young) girl wearing a gorgeous cardigan, with gorgeous bangles, gorgeous necklace and GORGEOUS handbag. It all inspired me to try harder to banish the witch, so early this morning I was out power-walking and did two circuits of the Oval (sports ground) and one circuit of the lake. It is surely better to be a thin witch than a chubby one. Wish I could get onto 'Australia's Greatest Loser' which starts next week.

Have been out to the mall this afternoon with Rebecca. We had smoothies and cakes at Michel's Patisserie – was delicious. Hope I don't have to get a job (but think I will probably need to before much longer) as adore this lifestyle of shopping and lunching. Actually, didn't buy anything today (except dog food) as being very good wife and watching the cents. Rebecca showed me a brilliant craft shop that sells material and sewing patterns. Wish my sewing machine would hurry up and arrive.

We had news the other day that our worldly goods have finally set sail on the Maersk Kushiro and are on their way to us. They are due to dock in Melbourne on 27 February. Hope my computer has survived the journey. We were warned that delicate goods can be damaged in heavy seas. Am keeping fingers crossed. Have been tracking on internet, but it's out of range at the moment so don't know where it's got to so far. Must say, am not very impressed with photo of ship – the pallets look to be rather exposed to the elements. Hope my photo albums and handbags are under cover or I shall be having a stern word with the Captain – wonder if he's got email?

Only one more night now and then my poor little girls are home again. There was a huge electrical storm here tonight – very scary. Massive downpour. Hope girls are undercover. On one of the nights, Annie was due to trek up-river in canoes and camp out in the bush, then make their way back to base next day. Hope it wasn't tonight. Feel overloaded with worry about them.

FRIDAY 1 FEBRUARY

My children are safely home – thank the Lord in heaven above. Cannot believe they are here. Will definitely have to give up diet coke now. Not another drop will pass my lips. Will consider moving onto Strongbow instead.

Spent the morning baking chocolate buns to welcome girls home. Also bought a new cake-plate to display them! It's called "Casa Domani" and is an imitation of Creamware, which costs a fortune back home. This was only $4.95. Australia seems to be rather big on cooking and baking, and you can get really nice items very cheaply if you know where to look. (It's a bit like fashion – if you're thin, you can buy really cheap stuff and still look great. Yet another reason to stick to my diet).

Lulu's coach was back first, at 2.45pm. When she climbed down the steps she looked a lot more confident than she had four days ago. Various girls shouted "bye" to her, and one gave her a hug. She said they all seemed very nice and a couple of them live on Harrington Park. The activities were not too daunting, although the caving was too much for her, as was the abseiling, but she had a go at everything else. She had been very cross to note that, although the showers only had cold water, the facilities DID include electrical points and she could have taken her straighteners. (Apparently, one of the teachers took hers!) She did flout the no make-up rule though, as I noticed she was wearing mascara when we picked her up. Obviously, I didn't frisk her baggage well enough when she left.

Annie's coach arrived back at 4.40pm, and she has also been ok. She hated every single activity, but got on very well with a group of girls. She did sit by herself on the outward journey, but said she was ok about it. She met a boy who has a cavalier like Jasper, and who refers to the dog as his "brother" – a kindred spirit!

Apparently, the caving was every bit as terrifying as I imagined, and Annie refused to do it. Three other kids also refused. One girl went in, but froze in terror and had to be coaxed back out again. The gap you had to squeeze through was tiny. Am very glad she didn't go in. The poor girl has got the biggest blister I've ever seen, on her foot, and she has sunburnt knees from the afternoon in the canoe. Lulu saw a snake and lots of bugs and lizards but her sister didn't see anything too scary. They both jumped straight in the shower and are now getting re-acquainted with their GHDs.

The other news today is that I drove the truck! Just to the Plaza to buy some margarine for baking. Husband was sitting beside me to supervise, and Jasper Conran was navigating. Luckily, there was minimal traffic on the road, and carpark was almost empty, so didn't cause any havoc. The husband says he's going to apply for my licence. Am hesitating for two reasons. Firstly, because I really, really don't like driving, and secondly because you have to have your photo taken – if it's a bad photo I will be stuck with it for goodness knows how long. Will probably have to show willing and get the licence though, if only to drive back from the pub so the husband can have a drink. Will also stop me from drinking too much Strongbow.

(Forgot to say earlier – Annie spotted some Gripples on a fence surrounding a cattle field in the wilderness! Also forgot to say that First Aid training partly consisted of instructing the kids to scream for help very loudly if they saw a snake!)

SATURDAY 2 FEBRUARY

Horrible day today. Shopping for school shoes – need I say more? Girls are under the impression that I have PERSONALLY requested the school to have such strict dress rules in order to provoke maximum annoyance of teenage girls. It's all MY fault that the only shoes allowed are flat, black lace-ups. We had the BIGGEST row, and I shouted at them in the middle of the shop!

After shoes, we then had to buy lunch boxes and pencil cases. Lulu wouldn't have a pencil case from Target or BigW (gross, apparently) but had to have a Hello Kitty pencil case from a market stall (3 times more expensive, but worth the money to end the stropping and sulking). We also need to buy her lots of very expensive art materials, but I decided it would be sensible to wait until school have confirmed she can definitely take the subjects she's chosen. Am absolutely sick to death of spending money on school items. The camping equipment cost an arm and a leg, the school uniform was completely extortionate, and now we've discovered that we're not eligible for the free school bus pass! Will be glad to get them to school on Monday and see something in return for all this outlay.

Against my better judgement, I have allowed Lulu to take both 'Visual Arts' and 'Design & Technology.' I did feel that one of those choices should have been more academically orientated, eg Commerce, but decided that it was better to let her study the subjects she is interested in, rather than make her do something against her will. She's promised to get her head down and work hard – but this child is very good at promising, yet not delivering! I shall have to crack the whip and keep her nose to the grindstone.

Very busy tonight, hemming school dresses. It is taking forever. The dresses are SO flared that the hem is a million miles wide. Annie wants her buttons changing from green to black (this is allowed) and Lulu wants hers completely re-modelling (this is NOT allowed) – she says it's too long, too flared and too loose-fitting. Afraid she will be deeply disappointed because I'm only going to alter the hem. Will brace myself for yet another row.

Looking forward to tomorrow. Going back to Shellharbour for another picnic and browse around the lovely shops. Hope girls might go for a swim in the pool, but not holding out much hope as they don't like getting their hair wet after they've spent hours straightening it. Am desperately hoping they will relax this high-maintenance grooming routine before much longer.

By the way, we're all worried about Jasper Conran. (I'm worried about his health, and the husband is worried about a possible vet bill). I think he's been bitten on his right front knee, and he seems to have made it bleed a little by biting it. He doesn't like me touching it, but if it's no better tomorrow I will have to pin him down and inspect it more closely.

SUNDAY 3 FEBRUARY

Better day than yesterday. Husband made the picnic again (he's really good at it now) and we went back to Shellharbour, as planned. Lulu wanted some new trainers (Xmas money) so we went back to the cool surf boutique. After trying on a million pairs, she settled on some white DCs. Husband nearly fainted at the price ($129.00) but it was her money, not ours. They put her in a good mood, so were definitely worth it!

Also went back to the wonderful trinket shop called Harbour Rose. Now, I've been in lots and lots of shops in my career as a Professional Window Shopper, but this is probably one of the best I've ever seen. It's absolutely crammed full of glittery, sparkly trinkets and clothes. The costume jewellery was out of this world and not TOO expensive, although didn't dare ask to buy anything. Still trying to wean myself out of the 'holiday' frame of mind where you feel it's practically compulsory to buy a souvenir (eg, handbag or jewellery) everywhere you go. Shellharbour is only an hour away and we can go anytime, so have to pace my shopping over the coming months and not rush to buy something every time we visit.

The shop also sells soaps, body lotion, handbag mirrors, perfume, fridge magnets, writing paper, handbags, notebooks, pictures, shoes and, best of all, silky, shimmery, glittery dresses and tops. The clothes are absolutely unbelievable, and there was a sale on! Lulu had her eye on a navy blue silk mini-dress, but she'd spent enough for one day so didn't encourage her.

On the way back up the coast we called at a resort called Bulli, and parked next to the beach to watch the surfers. There was a bit of a commotion going on at the car parked next to us. A girl was wrapped in a towel and crying and shaking, and as we listened in to the argument (we all lowered our windows) we gathered that the girl had almost drowned and the boyfriend wasn't terribly bothered about it. He never spoke while she was wailing on, but just calmly lit a cigarette and handed it to her!

We were all fascinated by the surfers. The waves were absolutely massive and you can't imagine that anyone would survive out there in the middle of them. I don't even need to mention the sharks. Once the surfers manage to stand up on their boards, it's very exciting watching them in action – one wave can bring them in from miles out at sea, right up to the beach. Could have watched them all night. The surfer boys are very talented at their chosen sport, but hope my girls never date any of them!

We had a laugh on the way to Shellharbour when girls were talking about their camping trip and Annie admitted that she'd dropped her water bottle and it rolled down the mountain and wedged in a tree. The leader had to go and fetch it for her (am pleased he did as it cost $29.00). She also re-told the swamp-wading tale. When they were canoeing, they hit a swamp and the canoes started sinking so they had to wade through and drag the canoes behind them. When I asked how the leaders could be sure there were no snakes or anything equally nasty in the swamp, the reply was that they couldn't! The poor child. I really admire her for managing to do it all because she's not exactly an 'outdoors' kind of girl. Take her 50 metres from her GHDs and she panics. Very proud of them both.

Girls have packed their bags ready for school tomorrow. Their father is taking them on the first morning, and after that they're on their own. They have to get the bus home tomorrow and haven't got time to hang around. Lessons finish at 2.40pm and the bus leaves at 2.45pm. Lulu will have no time for daydreaming – there is no other bus after this one!

Pleased to report that Jasper Conran's knee looks a lot better, thank heavens. He's stopped biting it, and he managed to terrorise the seagulls this afternoon so I think he's back to normal.

Forgot to mention earlier – as we were driving to Shellharbour we passed an enormous sign which read, "BEWARE OF WOLVES." As you can imagine, I was in absolute panic and screamed a little. I made sure all windows were fully wound up and doors firmly locked. Husband made a few jokes (which I did not find very funny) about going off the main road and into the wilderness to see if we could spot a few. I hysterically told him not to be so stupid and to stick to the main road. As we drove a few hundred metres further on, we passed a large football stadium, and it became apparent that the 'Wolves' were the local football team! Have made new resolution to stop over-reacting. Really MUST calm down. Will begin tomorrow.

WEEK 5
Roll With It

MONDAY 4 FEBRUARY

Girls have finally gone to school – halleluja! Had to thoroughly frisk Lulu before we left, and what a good job I did. The illegal haul included one necklace, two bracelets and a ring. Then when we were standing in Reception, it transpired that she'd 'customised' her backpack by removing the regulation waiststrap! She'd also rolled her socks down as low as possible. As soon as we arrived, a girl came rushing up to take charge of Lulu, and this girl looked like her clone – tall and thin, dark hair, socks rolled so low you couldn't actually see them! Annie was sent off to find her own way to her classroom, which was rather daunting, but just as she was about to set off a girl came up and offered to show her where to go. Was very hard leaving them, and am worried about them getting to the bus stop on time tonight. Will walk down to Harrington Parkway to meet them, and take Jasper Conran if it's stopped raining.

Before we left the school we called in at the Uniform Shop to see if the blazers were ready, but unfortunately not. While we were under the impression that the seamstress lady in the shop was just taking the sleeves up and altering a couple of buttons, they have actually been sent back to the manufacturer for 're-constructing.' Goodness only knows what the bill for that will be.

On way out of school, the eagle-eyed husband spotted that the Headmaster's car has a private numberplate which sports the school initials. This provoked a few choice comments about the cost of private education!

Didn't sleep very well last night. Keep having nightmares that someone is shaking me, and I wake up with a start. I can actually FEEL their hand on my shoulder, pushing me. One night last week I shouted at the husband because I thought it was him! I've been sleeping without any duvet covering me because it's so hot at night, and this morning I could feel the hand shaking my leg as I woke up! Hope I get over this soon as I really don't like it. Think maybe it's just the strangeness of everything that's playing on my mind a bit. Or maybe this is how madness starts! I don't feel too worried about anything here, definitely not having any regrets at all, but suppose I am very worried about the UK house not selling, and I was absolutely worried sick while girls were at camp. Doesn't help when the husband watches the "Flying Doctor" tv series and this week the doc flew out to tend to a little boy who lived on a remote farm in the bush. The boy had been asleep in his bed when a cockroach climbed in his ear and they couldn't get it out! Have instructed the husband NOT to repeat any more of these stories to me in future.

Feels very strange being in house by myself (and Jasper Conran) with a full day stretching ahead. Intended to go jogging round the Oval, but weather not good as been raining all night and still pouring down. Lots of laundry to do though, mainly girls' stuff from camp, and will make shepherd's pie for dinner. Thought shepherd's pie and Yorkshire puddings would make them feel at home after long first day at strange new school. Might also fit in a little nap as been up since 5.00am.

Little nap didn't work out very well, as Jasper Conran wouldn't settle down. Also, I was scared of not hearing the alarm and missing the school bus, as girls don't know their way across the estate yet. However, with hindsight I think they would have preferred me to miss it – as mentioned earlier, it has been raining all night and all day, and we don't possess a raincoat or umbrella between us. So, I ended up standing at corner of road, completely bedraggled and soaked to the skin. I looked like some old bag lady and definitely NOT the chic, cosmopolitan Sydney-dweller I had in mind when I moved here. My hair was plastered to my head, glasses were steamed-up and clothes were clinging to me. Girls disowned me as soon as they stepped off the bus, and walked a mile behind me. MUST work on becoming more elegant and graceful. Realised yesterday that I clamber in and out of the truck like an old farmer. Need to be more like Meryl Streep in "The Devil Wears Prada." She 'reverses' into the car seat, bottom first, and then swings her legs round. Not really possible I suppose, when the seat is above your waist-line. Will have to work it out. Perhaps next company car should be a low-slung sporty number. Will work on persuading husband to have a word with the boss.

Embarrassing mother notwithstanding, girls seem to have had a good day at school. Lulu had a slightly sheepish grin as she didn't like admitting that she'd enjoyed it. Every other Monday morning she has double maths for first lesson – will look forward to getting her up on time on THOSE mornings! There are four girls who are all best friends and appear to have embraced her as one of their group. Annie knows one of the girls in her 'Home Room' as they shared a tent at camp, so that was good. They hung around in a big group of about 10 girls at 'recess' and invited Annie to tag along with them. Two of the girls usually get the Harrington Park bus, so she will have someone she knows on the journey. She had some maths homework to do tonight, so that was very grounding!

Shepherd's pie and Yorkshire puddngs were a big hit tonight, made a nice change from 3 weeks of salad. Even the 'Gravox' gravy turned out ok. Better than the 'Clive of India' mustard powder I used in a recent macaroni cheese – girls thought I was trying to poison them. Clive's yellow powder is obviously a lot stronger than good old Colmans.

After dinner, husband and I went to BigW in Narellan to buy three umbrellas. This is first step to acquiring more poise. Simply cannot trundle around like a drowned rat any more. While we were out, husband and I discussed the 'Housekeeping Money Issue' and agreed on $250.00 per week, to be handed to me every Monday. This is for me to feed the family and give the girls an allowance. So pleased this is settled. I can feed the family on egg and beans every evening and thus have lots of money left over for Clarins beauty products. There are now five $50.00 notes staring at me as I type. Feeling very giddy.

TUESDAY 5 FEBRUARY

Thank goodness the rain has stopped, or at least slowed to a drizzle. When I took Jasper Conran out last night there was practically a river running down the street. There are massive storm drains built into the kerb at the corner of every street, with a notice saying, "THIS OUTLET DRAINS TO NARELLAN CREEK." There are even drains set into the lawn in the back garden. When it rains here the lake and streams turn brown, which Annie informs me is due to all the soil washing into the water. Everything soon gets waterlogged because the ground is baked so hard that it can't absorb all the water, and there is nowhere for it to go. Luckily, on Harrington Park it all seems to be going into the drains. The architect obviously knew what he was doing. According to the brochures, the estate was planned by Taylor Woodrow.

The land upon which Harrington Park is built used to be cow pastures, and it was owned by the Fairfax family. Apparently, Sir Warwick Fairfax was responsible for starting the Sydney Morning Herald newspaper. The family still owns a large chunk of land in the middle of the estate, known as "The Homestead." You can just see the original house through the trees, and I'm dying to go and have a proper look at it. It's private though, so not much chance of that happening – unless I can pretend to be a historical researcher!

Can't decide what to do today. Is 8.45am and have been up since 6.00am. Girls went off to school quite chirpy today. Lulu regaled me at breakfast with tales of how you ARE actually allowed to wear make-up. In other words, "Well, you're not actually ALLOWED, but all the girls wear it and they get away with it." Have issued stern warning that there will be no weekly allowance if I catch her wearing black eyeliner to school.

Think I will take Jasper Conran for a stroll, then power-walk to the Plaza and buy chicken for dinner. Might be some new magazines in the supermarket – am now a woman of means.

It is now afternoon and wish to report that I did not buy any magazines. Am very thrifty housewife. (Also should report that there were no new ones in supermarket, suspect they'll all be out on Thursday).

Have been jogging round the Oval today. Managed two circuits and will do three circuits tomorrow. Must build up by one circuit every single day. Am feeling very, very restless and need to pour all my energy into it (which isn't a considerable amount, actually) and report on progress daily. Nearly time to go and meet the school bus. Feeling deeply offended, as this morning girls asked if I would wait halfway across the parkland to meet them. Like to think it's because they want to be independent, but fear it's just because they don't want friends seeing drowned rat of a mother again.

Girls home safely and had nothing to moan about. They texted to say they were off the bus and were walking through the parkland – were supposed to text when they got ON the bus, but were obviously trying to put as much distance between us as possible. Had only just reached the path when they appeared. Is lovely to see them walking across the parkland in their new dresses, ankle socks and black shoes, with matching rucksacks – they seem to have regressed about 5 years! They've just gone upstairs to get changed and I can hear a HUGE commotion in the bathroom. Apparently, Lulu has found a spider and is screaming for Annie to come and zap it for her. Chicken, salad, baked potatoes and garlic bread for dinner, then hoping we might go for out for a drive if the husband is in a good mood.

Didn't go out for drive tonight – husband very late home. He'd managed to get an appointment with some architect-type person who could only see him late afternoon, and apparently the meeting was well worth being late home for. Girls and I had dinner together then Annie and I bathed a very grubby Jasper Conran in the utility room sink. He wasn't very pleased about it, but has now forgiven us.

The husband is going into Sydney to meet the boss tomorrow.

Suspect there will be some mighty hangovers in the Waldorf on Thursday morning!

WEDNESDAY 6 FEBRUARY

Have been mercilessly duped by unscrupulous husband. Am very upset. Due to all the recent, unrelenting, rain, I mentioned last night that I need another clothes airer to cope with all the wet laundry. Husband replied that I must pay for it out of the housekeeping money. Am furious. Obviously, I didn't go far enough into the finer details of the 'Housekeeping Money Agreement' with him. I thought he looked a bit smug when I agreed to it. This is a major blow. Clarins products are expensive enough anyway, but they are completely out-of-reach when there are airers to finance as well. I think the sensible thing to do is to just not wash his shirts quite as regularly, so don't need the airer space. And maybe give him cheese on toast for dinner (have discovered that Heinz beans are quite expensive here). Hmm, wonder if there's anything else I can deprive him of? Will have a little think while he's away tonight.

THURSDAY 7 FEBRUARY

Had a long think and decided not to punish lovely husband. He works very hard for us, and he's only concerned that we're careful with money until the UK house is sold. Did, however, let Jasper Conran sleep on his pillow while he was away last night (which really annoys him). Have had other, more important things on my mind today. Have been involved in the dramatic rescue of a much-loved family pet – don't worry, it wasn't Jasper Conran!

When the husband came home at lunchtime yesterday to collect his overnight bag for Sydney, he mentioned that he'd seen a house for sale on Olsen Place. We really like these houses so we whizzed round there to have a look. Outside the house there was a really cute little white dog, and we were laughing because the cheeky little mutt stared us out! We came home and husband went off to meet the boss.

Later that night, about 7.00pm, I was taking Jasper Conran out for his evening walk when a lady in a blue 4x4 stopped to ask me if I'd seen a little white dog anywhere as hers had been missing since 2.30pm. It turned out that the missing dog was the cheeky little monkey we'd seen at Olsen Place, and she's called Tia. I said I'd keep a look out for her. Hurried home as it started to rain. Just got indoors when we had the most HORRIFIC electrical storm. It was really fierce and we were all terrified. Kept thinking about poor little dog lost in storm and felt upset all night. Just imagine if that was Jasper Conran. Would have been devastated.

Saw girls onto school bus this morning and came back to write a note to the missing dog's mum, offering to help look for her if she hadn't turned up. Dropped note through her letterbox and set off to walk to Plaza to buy dinner. On the way I passed a poster about the poor little missing dog, so I put the 'phone number into my mobile and went to the supermarket. Bought chicken (and magazine) and started to walk home. Was just crossing bridge when little Tia came BELTING down the middle of the road into the oncoming traffic. She was absolutely filthy, and panting and completely terrified. I called to her and tried to catch her, but she ran off. A man in a white van stopped and shouted that he'd been trying to catch her for ages, but she wouldn't stop so he was just following her. I told him she lived at Olsen Place, and he carried on following her. I rang Tia's mum and told her she was running about. Luckily, she only worked at the Plaza so was on the scene in 2 minutes, and went off up the road to look for her.

I crossed over the road to check if Tia had gone into the park. Took one step onto the grass and didn't realise it would be waterlogged, so therefore very slippery. My feet went flying, I landed on my back and went hurtling down the bank towards the creek. I was petrified and thought I'd end up in a snake-pit like Harrison Ford. My shopping was scattered and I had landed on the chicken. It was very squashed. I screamed a bit and a lady walking her dog asked if I was alright. Luckily, I came to a stop before I hit the water (or the snake-pit). I stood up and my back was covered in mud from head to toe. I scraped up my groceries (luckily, the magazine was zipped safely inside my handbag) and staggered back to the road. Was just going along Fairfax Drive when the white van man went past and shouted, "We got her," and put his thumb up. I smiled and waved, through my pain, and limped home.

Had a shower and threw clothes in washing machine. Laid down on sofa with Jasper Conran and Harpers Bazaar. Was 10th anniversary issue and nearly 500 pages long and packed with very glamorous pictures. Felt more than a little depressed. How did I end up going for a casual stroll to Plaza and come back covered in mud? There was even grass in my ear. This is not elegant, stylish or poised behaviour. Will have to come up with action plan to improve self very quickly. Girls are on the point of disowning me.

FRIDAY 8 FEBRUARY

Continued my love affair with David Jones by spending the afternoon at Macarthur Square. Browsed all the major brands of make-up and chic clothes, including Sass & Bide, Esprit and Witchery.

Purpose of visit to mall today was to search out lifestyle-enhancing books in Borders. This is first step towards taking self in-hand. Am determined to become chic, cosmopolitan, stylish Sydney-person, as seen at the moment only in my imagination. Found two relevant books; "How to be a Lady," and "L is for Lady." Worryingly, they were only one shelf above, "How to Trace your Convict Ancestors," (quite easily, apparently). Didn't purchase either of the books, as housekeeping budget not up to it, but have a plan. Will be very, very thrifty next week, as opposed to just very thrifty this week, and then next Friday will buy one of the books and the other one the Friday after.

While waiting for time to pass until next Friday, am going to concentrate very, very hard on getting into shape. Will exercise every single day and stick like glue to diet. Will report on progress every day. Haven't been able to jog for two days as the Oval has been flooded, but will hopefully be clear by Monday. Can't wait to get started.

Other reason for visit to mall today was because Annie has requested some navy blue nail polish, "preferably Chanel!" Wanted to look at Chanel polish myself as seen advertisement in magazine for chic pale pink polish called Ballerina. Found it straight away in the lovely David Jones, and was extremely impressed with it. However, not impressed with the price (over $30). The old me would have immediately caved-in to temptation, but am proud to report that did not succumb. Instead, I found a shop called Gloss which sells very adequate nail polish for only $3. Found a navy blue for Annie and a pale pink for me and honestly, they appear to be exactly the same shade as Chanel. Exactly. Again, am proud to report that still did not succumb, as decided that daughters must buy polish out of allowance. The old me would have just bought them as a treat, but have decided that girls must learn the value of a dollar. When they've tidied their rooms tonight they will get their $25 allowance each, and we can go back to Macarthur Square tomorrow and make their purchases. I have become excellent, example-setting mother. Although, obviously, don't want them following my example of how to roll down a riverbank.

SATURDAY 9 FEBRUARY

Oh my - have seen how the other half lives. Trip out to Double Bay today and is just too fabulous for words. The shops. The houses. The bay. The pool. Was all just wonderful. Am beginning to sympathise with the Macarthur MP who allegedly absconded to the coast after winning his seat – if you can afford to live by the sea, it would be criminal not to. (Actually, I don't mean that – he's a public servant and should be loyal to the people who elected him. But still, imagine owning a house at the coast and NOT living in it. Would be madness).

Anyway, girls tidied their rooms this morning and were given their allowance, then we set off. Drove by Darling Harbour first, and unfortunately ended up going through quite a lot of tunnels. There was a lot of hyper-ventilating in the front seat (me and Jasper) and a lot of scorn thrown around (by husband, Annie and

Lulu). They all seem to think that I am claustrophobic simply to cause them maximum annoyance. Was awful. Very relieved when we arrived at the bay. Drove by the waterfront for a while, and then managed to get a parking space so we set off to look at the shops.

Walked past some wonderful boutiques selling Chanel, Max Mara, Balenciaga, Jimmy Choo, Gucci etc. etc. Didn't venture into any of those as didn't feel I would pass as potential customer. Walked past restaurants with neat little box hedges outside, and a jeweller with a window full of huge, grey pearl necklaces.

Found a very up-market little arcade, and was just about to enter it when Jasper Conran decided he needed a poo – right in the middle of the pavement. Being a good citizen, I cleaned it up of course, but there were no litter bins around, so this meant I entered the chic little arcade carrying a bag of dog poo! All I could think was, "Here we go again, no style, no poise, no elegance." Roll on next Friday when I can get to Macarthur Square and buy that book.

The first shop in the arcade was a wonderful stationery shop, and girls and I were desperate to look round it. We left Jasper Conran with the husband, and the bag of poo by the step, and went inside. It was absolutely full of fabulous little notelets, invitations, pens, pencils, journals, notebooks, sealing wax, seals and about a million different types of paper. They also had some brilliant pens that were a leopard print design with a black silhouette of Audrey Hepburn on them – very ladylike! Didn't buy anything, as still being very thrifty housewife (actually, am very amazed at self-restraint) but was extremely cross later when the husband confessed that he was expecting to be dragged inside to pay for some cute little trinket – and he was willing to do so! Missed out big-time, but we can always go back. Will DEFINITELY go back.

Came out of stationery shop, picked up bag of poo, and carried on looking around. Was all quite overwhelming. Went back to truck and had a drive around the lovely streets. The houses, particularly the ones on the edge of the cliff with a bay view, were unbelievable. Had a look in an Estate Agent window and saw that one of the apartments was $5.5 million!

On way home, was thinking about life and suddenly came up

with a plan. Am going to make it my ambition to lose lots of weight, acquire lots of style, poise and elegance and then bathe my way around all the fabulous ocean pools on the Eastern Coast. Is like something out of a film. Actually, think there was a film on similar theme with Charlotte Rampling and some hunk who swam his way across America via private swimming pools. But this is very different. Will have friends and family hanging onto their computers, watiting for photos of me in every pool. A new one every Sunday! Will be famous. Must go and research swimwear. Must just state though, it will be one-piece costumes – DEFINITELY NOT BIKINIS!

SUNDAY 10 FEBRUARY

Decided I desperately need some bathroom scales. Cannot stick to diet and exercise plan without getting weighed on regular basis, so husband and I went to mall this morning to buy scales. Invested in huge, medical-type weighing scales with massive dial. Cruel husband wanted me to try them out in the shop, but I firmly refused. Will use them for first time in the morning. Am hoping that as we're in the opposite hemisphere to one which body is used to, and therefore in a different magnetic force-field, the new gravitational force will pull the needle nearer to single figures. Will see tomorrow. Think will be pleasantly surprised.

WEEK 6
Cabin Fever

MONDAY 11 FEBRUARY

No. No, no, no, no, noooooooooooooooooooooooooooooooo. How can this be? I weigh 5lbs more than when I arrived here. Suspect it might be related to the consumption of Australian crisps and choc-chip cheesecake. My theory on the different gravitational forces had absolutely no effect on the needle on those scales. Have remembered that I failed school physics exam – twice!

Was so appalled by weight that went out power-walking immediately. However, discovered that Annie had borrowed my white trainers for PE so was left with her black ones. Coupled with my navy cropped joggers and white legs, this was NOT a good look. I looked like the fat friend in 'Kath & Kim.' Passed lots of glamorous power-walkers on way. They all have lightly tanned, slim bodies, black joggers, white trainers, skimpy vest tops, cool sunglasses and i-pods. I did not measure up. Came back though the parkland feeling very disgruntled, yet again. Passed lots of school-run mums on the way. The Harrington Park mothers are very chic. Do not know how they manage to look so immaculately groomed at such an early hour. Will have to try harder tomorrow.

Stuck in now waiting for washing machine repair man. Damn machine broke down on Friday. The electronic dashboard kept saying there was a problem with the filter, so I cleaned it out only to discover a hairslide trapped in the mechanism. Machine is under guarantee so will have to pretend that I don't know what the problem is, and hope we don't get charged.

Guess what happened tonight. Tia and her family called round to thank me for helping to find her. Unfortunately, I was in the bath when they called, so didn't get to meet them. Her mum had bought me a scratch card and told Allan she hoped it would be as lucky for me as finding Tia had been for her. (Sadly, it didn't win anything). I will text her mum tomorrow. We are obviously kindred-spirited doggy people. I suspect Tia gets away with napping on the bed, just like Mr Conran.

Went to bed feeling a bit brighter tonight. Have stuck to diet ALL day. Didn't buy any goodies in supermarket – not even a magazine. Am amazed at hitherto well-hidden willpower. Thought of swimming at Shellharbour is keeping me going. Think would like a polka-dot swimsuit. Some nice ones in Harpers Bazaar.

Final news today is that the washing machine repair man charged me $113 for mending the machine. He found the hairslide immediately and therefore it was deemed to be a call-out charge. Just think of the treats I could have bought with that money. Could even have gone back to stationery shop in Double Bay.

TUESDAY 12 FEBRUARY

My days have fallen into a pleasing (for some) pattern. I get up, see the husband and girls off to work and school, spend all day washing, ironing, cleaning and tidying, the family return home and spend all evening making a mess then go to bed. The next day the cycle begins again. Am obviously fulfilling important societal function – that of a slave. Thank goodness I have my Fridays at the mall.

Girls went to school in sports gear today, as it's the dreaded Sport Tuesday. Last week's sport was cancelled due to rain. They have lessons all morning and then sport all afternoon. Annie and Lulu have chosen weight lifting. When I expressed surprise at their choice, they explained that it apparently involves being taken by coach to local gym and then hanging around the treadmills all afternoon, chatting! It would appear that no actual lifting of weights takes place. Makes sense now.

Went to Plaza very early this morning to get final ingredients for Annie's requested dinner of Chicken Fried Rice. Am trying to budget for every meal, but find that I need so many 'store cupboard staples' (professional term used on website called, "Beginner's Guide to Pantry Pride" – I really DO need to get out more), it's costing me a fortune whenever I try to follow a particular recipe rather than just making something like shepherd's pie or buying a BBQ chicken. Trying to stick to $25 per day. I get $250 per week housekeeping and give $25 each to girls, so this means that if I stick to $25 per day for food, I get $25 to spend at the mall on Friday afternoons. Am marvellous housewife. Wish it hadn't taken me 18 years to get there though.

WEDNESDAY 13 FEBRUARY

Have received photo of myself and chums at leaving party from lovely friend in UK. Photo is very nice and indeed is the only shot of self in existence of which I actually approve. However, looking at it makes me think, "what on earth happened to me in the last 5 weeks?" Must be the heat. And the humidity. Maybe it's the different water. Maybe the Australian crisps. Maybe the choc-chip cheesecake. Photo has focused me into looking ahead – can see myself in imagination, looking fabulous in polka-dot swimsuit at Shellharbour pool.

Must say, looking at photo also made me think that those Saturday afternoon blow-drying sessions at Koko were WELL worth the money. Think girls are despairing of my wild hair, as they have offered to spend their Saturday morning straightening it for me!

Bitter row with husband this morning, as I asked for his bank card so I could go to Camden and buy some material. He refused to hand it over and said we "couldn't be wasting money on stupid material." I was furious, and cried a bit. He then relented and BEGGED me to go and get some, but I refused. Have therefore cut off nose to spite face, but have gained marital high-ground so don't care. I only wanted a few scraps to make lavender bags or door stops.

Sulked off to the Plaza to buy ingredients for caramelised leek and ricotta cheese tartlet recipe for tonight's meal. Cheese and leeks only came to $5 and rest of ingredients were store cupboard staples – marvellous new money-saving system is working! God bless theorganisedhome.com

There are Valentine's Day cards and presents everywhere at the Plaza. Won't be celebrating as husband will be in Melbourne, but as not actually friends with him at the moment, possibly wouldn't be celebrating it anyway.

Got dressed-up today. The husband's boss's father called unexpectedly yesterday (to bring the husband a lawn mower) and I looked hideous yet again. Bet he thinks I'm a hideous old hag. So, got dressed today in black linen trousers, black tee-shirt and silver ballet flats. Also did hair and make-up. Can absolutely guarantee that won't see a single soul other than husband and children. Must not consider it wasted effort though. Am sure that truly elegant women go to this much trouble EVERY day. Is exhausting though. Was in shower at 5.45am.

No diary or emails for next couple of days, as husband, laptop and internet connection will be in Melbourne until Saturday morning. However, will we cope? There's bound to be an internet-related homework crisis.

SATURDAY 16 FEBRUARY

Was very, very ill while husband was away in Melbourne. Wasn't sure I would survive until his return. Had the worst ever case of Cabin Fever. Have never before been struck so severely. I was climbing the walls. Girls went to school at 7.10am, I tidied house, ironed laundry, walked Mr Conran, went for power walk – and still had about 6 hours left to fill and nothing to fill them with. If I'd had some material I would have done some sewing, but let's not go there again. Husband rang on the Thursday evening to say Happy Valentine's Day, but I just muttered at him and put the girls on. Was not in the mood to be lovey dovey.

Spent Thursday afternoon making lists of menus and planning the weekend grocery list. Have voluntarily cut the housekeeping allowance to $200 in effort to save more money. We've discovered an Aldi near us, and it's far cheaper than the other supermarkets. There appears to be only two main supermarkets in Australia – Woolworths and Coles, and I find them expensive. Aldi seems to be much cheaper, and I only spent $94 this morning. All I need to buy at the Plaza next week is two BBQ chickens, bean sprouts and baked beans. I really HAVE become the best housewife.

Husband arrived home after lunch with a belated Valentine's card and a book (pity he hadn't left it for me to read while he was away). He dropped Lulu and I in Camden to browse for a couple of hours while he had a nap to recover from his night out in Melbourne. When he collected us, we decided to drive into Sydney and have a walk around the harbour. Well, words fail me once again. It was just TOO fabulous to describe. There was a massive cruise liner in the harbour at Circular Quay, and all the passengers were having dinner at a very swish restaurant on the harbourside. Jasper Conran was very over-excited. We walked right round the harbour to the Opera House, and were severely told-off by a security guard as dogs are not allowed on the famous steps. As it was a Saturday evening, a show was due to start and the crowd heading through the doors looked extremely smart. The women were all in slinky dresses and pashminas, and most were wearing diamonds or pearls!

We walked back round Circular Quay towards the truck, and were just going past the Hyatt Hotel when Jasper Conran had a bit of a panic attack. He's terrified of water and suddenly realised that he was on a decking walkway with water beneath him. He froze in terror and flattened himself to the floor. I had to pick him up and he cried in my arms. It amused the diners eating their romantic suppers under the huge white umbrellas.

Sometimes, I still can't quite believe we're in Australia. Walked around the harbour in a bit of a daze. It was a beautiful evening and the scenery is just spectactular. How on earth did all this happen to me???

SUNDAY 17 FEBRUARY

Had an exciting day. Am making a patchwork quilt and have found a new aspirational icon – Olivia Walton (of Walton's Mountain fame). If anyone dares to suggest that I have more in common with Grandma Walton, they will be in BIG trouble with me. Have finally made the husband understand that I need something to do, so he dropped me at the mall with $50 in my purse. Obviously, $50 doesn't buy very much, so needed to make it stretch as far as possible. Luckily, there was a sale in the sewing shop – all the quilting material was half price so I bought some lovely bright pink cotton, and then spotted the same pattern in lime green and thought it would make an ideal patchwork quilt for Lulu. So that's my project. When the girls have gone to school tomorrow, Jasper and I are going to sit out on the balcony and sew. Only thing is, husband is working from home tomorrow and when he's in the house during the day, I always feel that I should be doing housewifely chores. Will just have to front it out. Do, however, need him to sweep down the balcony for me first, and ensure that all spiders are eliminated before I venture out.

Apart from the quilting news, the other exciting news today is that while I was at the mall I also bought the "L is for Lady" book. Haven't had time to read it yet but will have a look tomorrow, straight after my weighing session – won't sleep tonight for worrying.

(Just before I go, should probably confess here that I also bought a bottle of nail varnish from Gloss. Was only $3.00. I bought the lovely 'Pink Manicure.' Have resolved to keep nails neat and glossy at all times. Up to now have been wearing 'White Beige' by Estee Lauder which was very popular a couple of seasons ago (worn by Gwynneth, allegedly) but am bored with that now. There appears to be a very fine line between 'ladylike' and 'fuddy-duddy' and have realised that it's very important to be on the right side of that line, no matter how faint it appears to be. All very confusing.

WEEK 7
Vicious Tongues

MONDAY 18 FEBRUARY

Went to bed a little perplexed last night, but couldn't quite put my finger on exactly what was troubling me. It wasn't just the worry about the weekly weigh-in. Couldn't drift off to sleep for ages, but was just dropping off when it came to me – if I sit out on the balcony sewing all day, I really will be like Grandma Walton. I might as well be sewing on the porch in my rocking chair. I need a more sophisticated hobby. Will just finish the patchwork quilt though, and then look for something more elegant.

When the alarm went off at 6.00am this morning, I was exhausted and could barely drag myself out of bed. However, girls have come to expect omelette and baked beans for breakfast every morning and I couldn't possibly let them down. Waved them off to school, then went back to bed for a nap. I obviously managed to get over my phobia about doing nothing when the husband is working from home because when I woke up again it was 11.30am! Decided to get the weigh-in over with, so gathered all my courage and stood on the scales. I HAVE LOST 5LBS! Couldn't believe it. Although, have been very, very good, so it was only fitting I lost quite a lot. Need to increase exercise regime this week, in order to capitalise on excellent result.

Managed to find time this afternoon to have a quick look at my lady guide. It is a very interesting book. I will definitely be more ladylike when I've finished it. The various chapters deal with issues such as conversation, deportment, entertaining and career. (Suspect I won't need the last chapter as it's about etiquette at work, and I've discovered there are absolutely NO suitable jobs out here in the countryside. Also, do not really need any advice re romance in the workplace!)

Will start working through the chapters in numerical order tomorrow, but today skipped straight to the page dealing with the car issue, as am determined to banish the lumbering old farmer. The section lists five steps on how to exit a car in style. The author obviously assumes the person striving for ladydom has no brain, because Step One instructs you to open the car door! Anyway, I read all the steps very carefully, and it would appear that Meryl Streep has also read them because it describes EXACTLY how she deals with the car manoeuvre in The Devil Wears Prada. As I don't have a Daimler-type vehicle like Meryl, I went outside to practice in the truck. Had to adapt the technique quite a lot actually, due to height of seat, but think the end result was definitely more farmer's wife than farmer!

TUESDAY 19 FEBRUARY

Jasper Conran is the defenceless victim of a cruel woman with a vicious tongue. Was walking round the lake today when a lady pushing a little baby in a pushchair stopped to chat and admire Mr Conran – or so I thought. She said how lovely he was and then asked if he was a 'pure-bred' cavalier. When I replied that of course he was, she answered, "It's just that he's so much fatter than all the other ones I've seen!" I was deeply affronted on his behalf and tried to explain that because he hasn't been clipped for three months, his fur adds at least an inch to his girth, but she looked very sceptical. I was tempted to say something about her fat baby (his arms and legs were MASSIVE) but couldn't bring myself to be so cruel. Am going to look for dog groomer immediately, in order to ward off any further comments.

I realised today that Annie doesn't fully understand the danger of snakes. When I told her that if she saw one on the path she would have to turn back, even if she would be late for school, she replied that if she was confronted by a snake she would just "step over it!" I was horrified and made her promise never to do this. In the words of the Snake Man who has a regular column in the Camden Advertiser, "A snake bite is very painful, it don't exactly tickle." Have bought a book from BigW entitled "How to Treat Bites and Stings," as I thought it best to be prepared with first aid knowledge, but to be honest I can't bring myself to look at the pictures in it. Have scared myself silly and probably won't sleep again tonight.

It was Sport Tuesday today, and once again girls appear to have enjoyed themselves. Annie had to work hard at the gym, but she had a good time, and Lulu had a brilliant time because she was chosen to officially miss all the activities. Apparently, the group was too large for the equipment available so the trainer asked for volunteers to help with a mailshot instead. Annie said that Lulu's group shot across to him so fast that no-one else stood a chance! She spent a pleasant afternoon folding mailshots and stuffing envelopes, and was rewarded with a protein bar!

Began reading the first chapter of my Lady book tonight, but was too tired to concentrate. Just managed the advice on how to brighten someone's day with a kind comment. However, the phrases are just not applicable to my limited social circle and are definitely not applicable to the rude woman at the lake. Too tired to concentrate. Sophistication will have to be postponed until I have more energy, but I'll bear the advice in mind when I go jogging.

WEDNESDAY 20 FEBRUARY

I have been SO sophisticated today. Was going out with Rebecca so decided to make a supreme effort. Was up and making pancakes at 6.00am. As soon as girls and husband left, I enjoyed a leisurely bath and then spent ages deliberating upon make-up. Read the other day that you should only apply colour to the top half of your eyes, never below the bottom lashes as it 'drags your face down.' Well, I definitely need my face lifting UP, so decided to give it a go. Also read that dark colours age you and light colours knock off the years, so again was more than willing to try it. Applied Clinique taupe shadow to the upper lids, and forced myself not to apply my favourite Nars 'Ashes to Ashes.' Have to admit the end result was very pleasing. Applied loads of mascara (Benefit) but couldn't quite bring myself to leave out the black eyeliner. If I keep up this beauty regime, I won't need to go and buy the Bobbi Brown eye-palette that I've been coveting. New look will save money in addition to knocking off the years and bringing me instant sophistication.

After make-up I blow-dried hair instead of leaving it to dry naturally (and frizzily). Then finally, I cranked up the neglected GHDs and subjected hair to punishing straighteners. The final touch was 'Pink Manicure' on my fingernails and I was ready to go. Went to look in full-length mirror and was taken-aback with surprise – actually looked more than passable. Think I might be on the road to becoming the lovely Samantha instead of Endora. Went out to meet Rebecca with a very light spring in my step. Will persuade the husband to go out for a drink tonight, as would be a shame to waste my new look just sitting around the house. Will have to think about what to drink though. Is not elegant to drink gallons of Strongbow. Wonder if my new bible advocates a ladylike drink? (Have just had a quick look, and it seems to recommend drinking cocktails or champagne – budget will not stretch to this, so it might have to be Strongbow after all, will decide when I get there).

THURSDAY 21 FEBRUARY

Very quiet day today. Slight headache due to excessive intake of Strongbow last night. Very cross with self. Spent all morning sewing on the balcony, with Jasper Conran snoozing by my feet. Am a bit worried. Feeling more and more like Grandma Walton and almost found myself saying, "You old fool, Zeb Walton," when the husband tried to kiss me goodbye this morning. Must focus on becoming more like Samantha, as she and Darrin were always very lovey-dovey.

Having settled upon new look with regard to make-up, decided to carry out inventory of my precious (dwindling) stock. Am worried about foundation as lately my trusty Benefit base is looking far too pale. I must have gained some colour in my face, despite copious amounts of sunscreen applied every single morning. Recently read an interview with Nicole Kidman (carried out on the set of her new film in Northern Australia) which states that her top beauty tip is "stay out of the sun." However, this is easy for her to do, as on-set there is a member of staff assigned the responsibility of following her around with an umbrella whenever she leaves her trailer. Lucky girl.

Inventory of make-up revealed rather a lot about my character – it is totally neutral! Possess three expensive eye-shadows which are all exactly the same colour. Why did I not realise this at time of purchase? Also, have rather a lot of eyeliners which are now deemed too ageing. Will pass them to outstretched hands of darling daughters.

After whittling down an array of identical lipsticks, am now in possession of pared-down beauty kit, which bestows maximum effect while looking natural and sophisticated. Am so pleased that time taken to get ready in morning has been sliced in half (although, will need that saved time to put extra effort into hair-taming procedures).

Looked in mirror today and could definitely see a difference in weight, although am a bit worried as fat seems to be disappearing from face and shoulders, instead of stomach. Still, is early days yet (11 to be precise) so will have to be patient. Can FEEL the chic Sydney-girl bursting to get out. At least now she seems to be waiting in the wings, instead of hiding behind the scenery stuffing her face with popcorn!

FRIDAY 22 FEBRUARY

Just love my new life. Husband working from home again, so he gave me a lift to Camden this morning, then collected me again a few hours later. Had a brilliant time. Found lots of new shops and a wonderful old-fashioned deli/café where I had a prawn sandwich and a glass of iced water. Also found a really great second-hand bookshop and a fabric shop which sells Vogue patterns. Camden is just so wild west, I almost expect to see a sheriff riding down the street! Talking of sheriffs, the policemen here appear to carry guns – is very scary when they stride past you (and a little bit sexy, to be honest!)

Annie has gone out to the movies with a friend tonight. The husband, Lulu and I drove to Borders in Parramatta to collect a previously ordered "To Kill a Mockingbird' dvd which Annie is studying for the School Certificate. While we were in Borders, I noticed a greetings card which read, "I have bursts of being a lady, but it doesn't last long!" It's a quote by Shelley Winters, apparently. Hope my conversion to Ladydom is not as fickle as Shelley's – once I get there, I'm planning to stay!

SATURDAY 23 FEBRUARY

Was a bit disappointed today. Two huge cruise liners (QE2 and Queen Victoria) are due in Sydney harbour this weekend, and we were going to go down and watch them arrive. Had planned to wear lovely Boden jacket (xmas present to self, as yet unworn). However, there was a radio announcement that warned the last time one of these ships docked at the harbour, the whole of central Sydney came to a standstill and roads were gridlocked. Apparently, families were stranded for hours, so we decided not to go. Lovely Boden jacket is still unworn.

Nothing much happened today. Had a severe tongue-lashing from the husband who told me off for wasting water (was only washing-up, but is apparently not acceptable to rinse plates before filling sink). Is on news though about how the dams are fuller than they've been for years. And all the neighbours are constantly watering their lawns under cover of darkness. The highest status symbol around here appears to be a lush green lawn!

Is now almost 10.00pm, just got back home. We've been for a ride out to Cronulla to watch the surfers. Was a beautiful evening and we played Van Morrison full-blast all the way. Waves were HUGE tonight, and very scary. Some of the surfers were really far out to sea. Sky was so clear we were able to watch all the jumbo jets dropping down into Sydney (relieved I'm on the ground, and not in one of them). Drove home in dark along the highway, not the lonely kangaroo road. Think we're staying in tomorrow as girls have homework and revising. Was thinking on way home, must not dwell on amusing Shelley Winters' 'lady' quote. Must remember she was an obese actress who never conquered her weight problems. Not a good role model. Must forget about her. Even if she did save the day in The Poseidon Adventure.

SUNDAY 24 FEBRUARY

Very cross with Annie today as she has left revising for a Business exam until the last minute. Need to keep a closer eye on her. Lulu has been painting yet again. That art book will be full before long. She does some very nice work, but I would prefer to see her doing maths revision. Am checking school diaries every single night now, to make sure they're both keeping up-to-date.

Weigh-in day tomorrow, and I can't wait. Jeans are far too big for me now, and I'm looking forward to buying some new ones. They were always a disaster though. I bought them in October when I was in a massive hurry, and chose the first pair I spotted in my (generous) size. It wasn't until two days later when I was rushing down the street as I was late for an appointment that I realised they were actually flecked with gold glitter and look very similar to the (much smaller) jeans I wore to the Church Youth Club circa 1979! Always being on the verge of losing masses of weight though, (only in my mind, up to now) I just put up with them, thinking it would only be for a few weeks. Will look forward to throwing them in dustbin – better not burn them out here, there are very large fines for starting a fire!

WEEK 8
Bad Mother's Day

MONDAY 25 FEBRUARY

YES, YES, YES – have lost 4lbs. That makes 9lb total weight loss. New jeans here I come. Not this weekend though, think will wait another two weeks. I want cropped jeans to show off all my fabulous sandals. Up to now have been mostly wearing silver ballet flats, but they're almost dead and ready for the dustbin. Very happy with the Lady in the mirror today. I look rather slim from the head-on view, although still very portly from the side angle.

TUESDAY 26 FEBRUARY

Very quiet day today. Went on spider patrol this morning and carried out a minor massacre.

As you walk around Harrington Park, what really stands out is that every single house is absolutely immaculate. All the windows, doors, gutters, fences etc. are clean and shiny. I think it must be to keep the spiders under control. You only have to relax for half a day, and they overrun the garden again. Most of the fences here are corrugated metal – termites eat the wooden ones – and the spiders like to make cosy little homes in the corrugated grooves. I hadn't really noticed them at first, but once you do see them you just can't forget them.

On the second day here I found a massive redback on the patio. So, this morning I went out with my can of 'Mortein' spray and blasted all the spiders on the fence into oblivion. Inspected them an hour later and they were all dead in their webs.

WEDNESDAY 27 FEBRUARY

Walked to the Plaza very early this morning to buy bread and milk, and was almost caught up in a fierce bird fight! The parrots were having a real set-to, screaming and fighting and swooping. Still find it surreal to see parrots and budgies flying free; they appear to have a wonderful life.

Received confirmation today that our Medicare health cover has been accepted. This is (I think) the Australian version of the NHS, under which we are entitled, as British Citizens, to receive 'reciprocal healthcare.' You wouldn't believe the form-filling and information that's been requested. Husband has handed over copies of our passports and visa numbers about five times now, and they STILL wanted additional proof that we were actually resident in England. We should have our Medicare cards in a couple of weeks, and not a moment too soon as I'm running out of thyroxine.

Spent the morning virtual window-shopping for lovely clothes to fit my soon-to-be-svelte body. (Husband suggested my time would be better spent earning some money to pay for them!) I'm now officially addicted to Net a Porter. I've developed an obsession with Antik Batik clothes and have found a white blouse which I simply HAVE to have, but there's one big glitch. A ridiculous one. It appears that this blouse is available in small, medium and large, but the corresponding size guide informs me that small is for Bust 28", medium is 29" and Large is 30"!!! Feeling very cross as it's only £75 and I could pay for it with the money in our UK bank and have it delivered here. Would have been perfect for strolling around Manly and Cronulla on a balmy Friday evening. Or shopping in Double Bay on a Saturday afternoon. Never mind. Am no stranger to disappointment; in fact, we're intimately acquainted. Besides, husband would have killed me and I can't possibly die before swimming up the coast via glamorous ocean baths!

THURSDAY 28 FEBRUARY

Darla will be so proud of me. This week I have been the absolute epitome of a perfect housewife. Have made fresh, tasty meals all week. Made shepherd's pie on Tuesday and ensured one panful of meat filled two dishes, so we're having it again tonight, and I made the leftover meat sauce into another meal for Wednesday by serving it with jacket potatoes and salad. All this from one large tray of mince. Haven't had to buy any extra food during the week, for the first time since the Housekeeping Money System began. The Maersk Kushiro is due to dock tomorrow, so hopefully I'll soon be reunited with my Happy Housewives book, and then I'll be able to employ the rest of Darla's tips. (Have got nagging feeling on the edge of my consciousness that all this 'Perfect Housewife' stuff is merely distraction therapy, but who cares – it's better than working for a living!)

Annie had invited friends home tonight, as they all had to work on a project for PHSE. She told me not to bother making dinner for them, as she didn't think they would be here very long. However, I made mini pizzas, chocolate muffins and cheese scones – from memory! Just call me Nigella, Delia or Jamie. Nigella – ha – will soon be thinner than her!

Most important thing to mention about the baking is that it was all done by using my STORE CUPBOARD STAPLES! See what you can achieve if you have a system? If I get bored at home (not very likely) I can always get a job as professional housekeeper to rock star, actress or similar type of person.

The baking went down very well with friends, and a good job too, as they were here until 7.00pm. Lulu ended up making them some pasta as well. The girls were all very nice, and they have been very kind to Annie. They're coming again soon to finish off the project. Apparently, we live the most centrally for them all, one lives on 20 acres and has horses and a guest lodge in the grounds!

Have been slightly concerned about school. In Science this week, some of the girls were setting fire to their shoelaces, and in English some of the boys were escaping through the window and back in through the other side! Annie assures me the guilty perpetrators were severely punished.

Have been too busy this week to do much work on my etiquette project, so tonight I've been reading the chapter re hosting and dining etiquette. Very informative, and gave invaluable advice on scenarios such as how to tell someone they've got food stuck in their teeth, how to open a bottle of wine and how to taste wine like a pro. I now understand the rules of table decorum and how to use a napkin – NEVER TUCK IT INTO YOUR SHIRT!

FRIDAY 29 FEBRUARY

It has been a day of very mixed emotions. Started off well with my regular Friday jaunt to Camden. Had my usual prawn sandwich in the Gourmet Deli on Argyle Street, and this week I found a shop called The French House which sells beautiful fabric and trinkets. Also checked out The Beaded Bouquet which sells jewellery-making equipment. Was a lovely morning. However, I then went home and found a GIGANTIC redback spider in the utility room. I was petrified, and there was no Mortein spray left. Not a single can in the whole house. Luckily, I managed to kill it using a variety of methods. First I sprayed it will floor cleaner, then mashed it up with the sweeping brush and finally flushed it down the sink. Have sprayed floor cleaner all around the door frame, which is where it must have entered.

These damn spiders make me so jittery. If I've seen one, and dealt with it, I then find myself jumping out of my skin for the rest of the day. It's worst when I have a shower because all the tiles are white, with single black tiles in a random pattern. When I've taken my glasses off, I think that all the black tiles are spiders waiting to pounce. I also worry about them when I buy salad and vegetables. I'm an advocate of the Marks & Spencer school of shopping, where everything comes ready-washed in a plastic bag. I hate having to peel and wash and chop things, and am constantly on red-alert while doing so. I must stock up on Mortein spray tomorrow.

Next weekend the yearly Camden show is being held at the local showground. Lots of shops on Argyle Street are displaying memorabilia connected to Camden in the 'olden days.' One of the best windows is displaying some old telegrams, and one which made me laugh said, "FURNITURE ARRIVED FRIDAY. DOG ALRIGHT. LETTER FOLLOWING. LOVE. THANKS. SID." It was dated 1938. Old Sid must have been a dog lover, although doubt his dog was as cute as Mr Conran. Wonder if they had quarantine rules in those days?

SATURDAY 1 MARCH

We've been to Bondi beach today! Can't believe I walked along the famous sea-front. It was so achingly cool and I was not worthy of being there (in my baggy, sparkly jeans). You should have seen the Bondi girls. There were all wearing maxi-length halter-neck dresses, or cut-off shorts and bikini tops, with their hair in cool pony tails. I looked like a haggard old mother-type person next to them. Would have looked much better in the fake Ray-Bans I found in a gift-shop, but the husband was ignoring my hints. Lulu bought herself some huge bug-eye sunglasses with her allowance, so she looked even cooler than usual and she fitted right in with the locals. She browsed longingly in the Converse/Vans shoe-shop, but they were way beyond her means (and mine). She will have to save up for a few weeks and then we'll take her back to get some.

The waves at Bondi were absolutely awesome, but the beach was very quiet with hardly any sunbathers/surfers. It transpired that this was because there was a Mardi Gras Festival in the centre of Sydney, and I think everyone under 40 was gathered there. You wouldn't believe the sights we saw on the way home. I wanted to blindfold Lulu, who was in the front seat and had a birds-eye view of it all. Men were dressed as women, or nurses, and women were dressed as anything at all – most of them were wearing huge angel wings strapped to their back. We saw a group of men who were wearing leather chaps strapped to their legs AND NOTHING ELSE!!! The whole of their 'bottom area' was completely uncovered! It was very disturbing. The husband kept muttering,

"Their parents must be very proud of them," like an old man of 90!

Can't wait for Monday's weigh-in. I should hopefully have lost a stone by then. I wore my old baggy jeans to Bondi, as the black linen trousers are on the side of chic rather than cool. Double Bay may be only round the corner from Bondi, but there's a whole world of difference between them. To be honest, I'd rather be a Double Bay Lady than a Bondi Girl. Am far too old to be a cool Bondi-type. My gorgeous girls will fit right in though.

While typing tonight, I was interrupted by a HUGE spider crossing the floor of the study. I screamed and shouted for the husband to bring the new can of killer spray. The spider ran behind the bookcase so I couldn't get it, but when I went to the kitchen for a cold drink, it came out again. I managed to squirt it, but not before it scared me half to death. I got my reference book out and I think it was a Huntsman, although I can't be certain it wasn't a funnel-web. The book informs me that huntsman spiders are harmless. Well, I can tell you they may be 'harmless' in relation to the damage caused when they bite, but they are certainly not harmless in relation to the stress they put on my poor nerves. Going to lie down – after first checking under the bed.

SUNDAY 2 MARCH

Have had the worst day ever. Didn't know it was Mother's Day until very late last night when it was mentioned in a couple of emails from friends. Consequently, for the first time in 15 years, I had no card or presents. Lulu scribbled a very basic card, which took her all of 5 seconds. Australia doesn't appear to celebrate Mother's Day, although the husband's work diary sees fit to mention the birthday of HM the Yan di Pertuan Agona (Malaysian) and the Khao Phansa Day in Thailand.

Huge row with naughty children this morning, although it was not related to the lack of Mother's Day gifts. They were both told about 20 times to go and sort out their homework and tidy their bedrooms. They both ignored me about 20 times before I blew a fuse and whacked Lulu's backside with a magazine as she walked past me. I lost it with them when they started fighting in the spare bedroom and Annie crashed into the wall – it was a miracle she didn't go right through it, as the walls are only plasterboard.

Of course, as soon as I'd lost my temper they were both very smug as they then held the Moral High Ground, and instantly ceased fighting in order to bond together against the common enemy – me. I was so annoyed with them that I made the husband chauffeur me to Macarthur Square mall and I enjoyed a peaceful 4 hours by myself. Bought Harpers Bazaar and refuse to feel guilty about it. Am now not speaking to rude and thoughtless offspring, and have abdicated all child-rearing responsibilities for the rest of the weekend.

WEEK 9
Jasper Conran is a Smart Little Fellow

MONDAY 3 MARCH

Feeling slightly disappointed, but probably being unrealistic. Stepped on scales this morning and have only lost 2lbs. Reminded self that losing 11lbs in 3 weeks is a remarkable feat. Very cross with self because I had a 'Lost the Plot' day yesterday. Was so fed up with naughty children that I bought a huge bar of dairy milk macadamia nut chocolate. Was absolutely delicious, and although it was worth it at the time, it definitely wasn't worth it this morning. Won't lapse again. Going jogging round the Oval now.

Bit of a boring day today. Did all the laundry and tidied-up. Girls and husband came home and made a mess. Jasper slept all day as was very hot again. Weather is supposed to be cooling down as we're now into Autumn. People keep telling me that we've had a very mild summer – goodness only knows how I'll cope with a hot one!

Tried out my new foundation this afternoon. Bought it yesterday at Macarthur Square. Only $3.00 from Gloss. No more Estee Lauder or Benefit foundation for this poor housewife. Have to say though, it seems to be very good so am not bothered that it was cheap.

Drove up to Narellan with the husband tonight. Trying to work out if I can walk to the local shopping mall. Looks like it's possible, so am going to see if there are any jobs going up there. Am willing to do anything except serve chicken-necks at the butcher. Will type a new cv and leave a copy at all the offices in Narellan. Something might turn up. Will have to fit in with Jasper Conran though, as surely cannot just leave him in cage all day?

TUESDAY 4 MARCH

My faith in the lovely Australian people has been restored. Was down by the lake with Mr Conran very early this morning when an elderly man stopped to pat him and said, "What a grand little chap, isn't he a smart little fellow." I agreed that Jasper was indeed a grand little chap and a very smart little fellow, and was dying to complement the elderly gentleman on his sprightliness and his fine walking stick, but just stuck to saying thank you.

Despite meeting kind old man, am feeling a bit down today. Have got a rash all over my stomach and it's very uncomfortable, not to mention also a bit disgusting. Just when I thought I was recovering some composure, I take a step backwards. Also, am having bad reaction today to stuffing face with chocolate on Sunday – won't go into details, but suffice to say I spent a large part of the day in the bathroom!

Lulu came home tonight with scary tale about a snake in the school grounds. Was obviously a deadly one because the children were rounded up and herded to safety while one of the Agricultural teachers arrived with a special snake-catching implement. The snake disappeared under one of the air-conditioning units so Lulu didn't see the actual capture. She'd just recovered from the drama of the snake when someone spotted a large lizard in the maths class! And to think I used to die on the spot when there was a wasp on the bus!

WEDNESDAY 5 MARCH

According to Harper's Bazaar, I need to have a uniform. Apparently, identifying your 'personal uniform' is a concept that "tons of stylish women" employ. Considering that HB is probably talking about ultra-chic New York women here, this concept is fine by grungy old me. The theory behind it seems to be that you buy your 'uniform staples' from very expensive designers, as these core items do not change. Then you buy your accessories from the cheaper end of the fashion scale and update them all the time. Very sensible concept, although suspect that HB's idea of 'cheap' will be vastly different to mine. Will have serious think about new uniform, and debate the best time to break news to husband that I need to buy one.

I just LOVE the American edition of Harpers Bazaar. Despite the rather steep import price charged by Borders, it's worth every single dollar. For one thing, it inspires me to keep up with diet and exercise regime, so don't really consider that husband is justified in complaining about price of magazine when he's getting a new wife for just $14.95 a month. Complete bargain. He should be thrilled.

THURSDAY 6 MARCH

My housewifery skills know no bounds. I can create meals from nothing (or at least from very little). Have bought a cookery book entitled "Cheap Eats," and today followed the recipe for potato pizza. Girls loved it. Husband was less keen, but never mind. Also made bread today – delicious and cost practically zilch. Aldi flour is only 79c for a whole kg. Girls now take a tub of tuna and cucumber pasta for school lunch, and the Aldi pasta is again only 79c. To think of the money I wasted in Sainsburys. Have vowed to never again allow self to be wooed by corporate advertising. We're going to investigate "The Fruit Barn" in Camden at the weekend, as it appears to be very cheap. Note: the strenuous kneading of bread/pizza dough will be very good for toning arms, thereby saving on gym membership – see, cheap AND practical. I deserve some sort of medal for my outstanding housewifery. (Actually, would be very pleased if the medal could be a Chanel-type of necklace, rather than an actual medal – have seen one on Net-a-Porter).

Today I discovered charity shops! The St. Vincent de Paul Society is big business in Australia, and I can tell you they have some real bargains. I bought some books for Lulu (20c each) and a Vogue dressmaking pattern for 50c. It's for a boxy Chanel-type jacket and is very chic – let's hope my sewing skills can do it justice.

Having a break from routine tomorrow and going out with Rebecca instead of my solo Friday jaunt to Camden. We're going to Camden on Saturday though, as it's the Camden Show. At the end of Argyle Street is the Camden showground, and as we drove past tonight we could see all sorts of rides and sideshows etc. I've been on the website and the show looks like something out of Seven Brides for Seven Brothers – there's a log-chopping contest and a rodeo with a bucking bronco competition! Annie is going to the show with 3 or 4 girls from school, and she's invited Lulu to go with them.

FRIDAY 7 MARCH

It's now Autumn here so I think that means I can avoid the sunhat crisis until next summer, which I think is November. I will be very thin by then, so will be able to wear anything!

Went to Camden Tea Rooms with Rebecca this afternoon. Was very rural, but very nice (mistakenly ate a delicious caramel shortcake). Didn't get home until 3.30pm and had no dinner prepared, so we decided to buy fish and chips in Camden and have a look at the showground. However, show was far more expensive than anticipated, so we didn't go in. Decided we'd rather give the girls more money for them to spend at the show tomorrow. Very disappointed to miss the rodeo; you should have seen the cowboys – luckily, they were wearing jeans beneath their chaps, unlike the boys at last week's Mardi Gras!

SATURDAY 8 MARCH

Have been giving a lot of thought to my new uniform, and while I haven't definitely decided upon anything, I can tell you that Tods and Hermes both feature heavily. Will unveil the final list shortly.

Girls have gone to Camden Show this afternoon, to meet up with friends. Slightly nervous about leaving them, but they have mobiles so can ring if they need us.

I went to Camden this morning and did my usual jaunt of shops and lunch at the Gourmet Deli. While I was munching my prawn sandwich, and reading Vogue, I was eavesdropping into the conversation at the next table. The lady was explaining to her friend that they've had to get rid of their chickens because they attract mice and mice attract snakes. Apparently, she's got mice in her cavity wall and the snakes go into the cavity to get them! It gave me the shivers. Sometimes I feel very far outside my own personal comfort zone.

The husband and I have been very industrious around the home this afternoon. I made fresh bread rolls and salmon pasta penne for dinner, and he's been mowing the lawns and strimming the borders. Should point out that neither of us were this dedicated at home – think the change of scenery has been just what we needed, although would obviously prefer that scenery to be snakeless!

SUNDAY 9 MARCH

Has been a very busy day, with one thing and another. Firstly, got up this morning and decided to cut off the long, ratty bits of my hair. Annie was horrified, but Lulu egged me on – a huge battle was raging, with me in the middle holding the scissors. Annie made me reconsider and think about how I'd feel if it went wrong. She is very sensible child. Lulu wanted me to just go for it. She is very reckless child. In the end, Annie agreed that the long front ends were very dry, so I went for it and snipped them off. Thankfully, it worked out well and hair looks much better now.

The other monumental event is that I saw my first kangaroo today. Was a little baby Joey and very, very cute. Sadly though, it was dead by the side of the road and just looked as if it was asleep, poor little thing. Worryingly, it was only a couple of miles up the road from where we live, and there are NO kangaroo warning signs. Will have to keep eyes keenly on roadsides at all times now, as Australian signage system obviously cannot be relied upon.

Husband and I had a romantic day out by ourselves. We left Mr Conran and his sisters at home – girls supposedly doing homework, but in reality on internet and MSN. We went first to see some showhouses at a complex near Liverpool. They were utterly breathtaking, but cannot begin to dream about new house here while the UK house remains unsold. At a rock-bottom price. Amid a stagnant market.

Decided to go to Darling Harbour after house viewing, and stopped for delicious snack in a waterfront bar. We enjoyed BLTs and cool drinks at a table in the shade, and listened to the band playing old Police hits, while watching the speedboats and steamers sail past. Had to take another reality check and make sure it really is me living this life!

Just as we were about to leave, a party of six schoolgirls arrived at the table next to us. I think they must have been from a boarding school as they were all wearing (very short) checked school dresses and were accompanied by an older chaperone. Every single one of these girls was tall, natural blonde and very pretty. Made me wonder which school they were from and what the entry criteria was – perhaps blonde hair scores higher than the entry exams over here!

WEEK 10
Drudgery and Servitude

MONDAY 10 MARCH

Disastrous day. Began badly this morning when we slept in. Girls and I in mad panic, but husband very calm and supercilious. He did, however, graciously offer to give girls a lift to school. When everyone had left and I finally had time to look in mirror, I screamed in horror. It appears that I've been bitten on the end of my nose, slightly to the right-hand-side. Nose is bright red, swollen and infection has spread in a lurid stain right across the bulbous end. To make matters even worse, when I finally calmed down enough to face the weekly weigh-in, I had not lost a single pound. Not even an ounce. Am very, very cross with self. For eating BLT yesterday and maple syrup pancakes this morning. Must try harder. Must focus. Must ignore bulbous nose and concentrate again on self-improvement programme.

Completed a longer power walk today, in order to combat the fattening effects of the maple syrup pancakes. Sun was very hot, though, so also had a longer nap in order to combat the exhausting effects of the power walk. After washing, ironing and cooking for (ungrateful) family, finally sat down tonight with my L is for Lady book, and read the chapter dealing with posture and deportment. Learnt that my walk should be a combination of a geisha shuffle and a supermodel strut! It also advises that you practice in a reflective shop window. Cannot possibly do this, the people of Camden will think I am insane.

TUESDAY 11 MARCH

The main reason for coming to Australia was to lift the husband out of the rat-race and give him a new challenge after spending 30 years working in the UK construction industry. Well, it would appear that we've lifted him clean out of the rat-race and straight into the jet-set! He's out on the town in Sydney tonight with the Gripple chairman, staying in a boutique hotel in The Rocks, and having dinner in some fancy bistro. I went on the website for this hotel (The Russell) and the blurb kindly informed me that, "Ideally located in the heart of Sydney's historic Rocks area, this small boutique hotel will charm your socks off!" How did this happen? How come I've been lifted from a life of drudgery and servitude, straight into another life of drudgery and servitude? Still, as long as he's happy jetting around, then I'm happy on my balcony. I'd better go and get on with sweeping the floors and kneading the bread.

WEDNESDAY 12 MARCH

Bit of a drama this morning. Was just getting dressed when Lulu rang to say she had forgotten her bus pass and was halfway across the parkway. Had to go tearing down the road in jeans and pyjama top to catch up with her. Was so out of breath could hardly speak, but the look I gave her conveyed my feelings. She scuttled off and must have caught the bus because she didn't ring again.

Recovered from early morning sprint and walked to the Plaza to buy chicken. Took Mr Conran for his stroll and then hung about the house, doing ironing etc. After finishing chores, Jasper I sewed on the balcony for a few hours, then made dinner for girls. Husband rang to say he'd had an excellent night out and was nursing a bit of a hangover. Gave him no sympathy whatsoever.

THURSDAY 13 MARCH

Australian radio is great. The Hi-Lux is tuned into a station that seems to play only 70s and 80s music. On our drive out the other night we listened to Abba, Elton John, Leo Sayer, Kraftwerk and The Human League.

The other station programmed in by the husband is Sydney's version of Talk Radio. My favourite story on the radio tonight was about a woman from Brisbane who has been sentenced in court today for stabbing her husband after he banned her from listening to Bruce Springsteen! And she only got 8 years in jail. I've warned my husband to take heed of this case because I am forbidden to play Bruce Springsteen or Bryan Adams in the car, as he can't abide "wailing guitars" when he's driving.

FRIDAY 14 MARCH

Our worldly goods have arrived! There are 15 boxes in the lounge, containing the sum total of our lives so far. Everything else was sold, given away or thrown on the tip. Feeling a little bit worried actually, as am now the proud owner of nothing! Nothing to show for 18 years of marriage and 43 years of life. Having a major de-clutter was so liberating at the time, but the reality is that we've now got no money and no possessions. The few possessions we do have are a bit bewildering. Why did I ship an electric amp which doesn't work and a tenor recorder that Annie has not played in 5 years? I threw out a stainless steel designer kettle, yet sent over a Buddha head ornament which cost only £9.99. Actually, while my body was present during the packing, my mind was definitely elsewhere. The last two months in England were just a blur when I was trying to manage without the husband, with working every day, with two distraught children and with sending Jasper Conran across the world by himself. It was very stressful and I felt at breaking point every single day, so I cannot be blamed for making irrational choices in the packing department.

SATURDAY 15 MARCH

Very, very angry this morning. Took Jasper Conran to be clipped at reputable salon attached to local vet. Returned to collect him a few hours later and imagine my fury when the receptionist brought him back to me reeking of perfume and sporting silk bows in his ears! I was furious. The poor little boy was object of derision. Not going there again. Jasper obviously felt humiliated, as he laid down on floor of truck instead of looking out of the window as usual.

Girls had lots of homework to complete so after collecting Jasper, husband and I went for a drive down the coast. It's been a very hot day and it was a beautiful drive. As my cds have arrived (the only items worth keeping) we listened to The Beautiful South all the way. Went to Wollongong first to check out the ocean baths for the unveiling of my slim body next November. Then down to Shellharbour and yet another browse around Harbour Rose. Coveted some lovely 'diamond' earrings in pastel coloured pink, green and lilac, but managed to resist as need to purchase new anti-virus for computer – a boring but necessary purchase.

On way home I foolishly allowed husband to follow the 'Tourist Drive' back to Camden. Was very worried when the signs told us to follow 'Sheepwash Road' through to 'Kangaroo Valley.' Once again had eyes keenly fixed on roadsides for rogue hoppitty beasts, but didn't spot any. The Tourist Drive was quite scary in parts, mainly when it led us up a very steep mountain with sheer drops merely inches away from the left side wheels. My stomach kept flipping over every time I glanced down the valley. Very relieved to reach the top as the road just levelled out, rather than going back down again, and the rest of the drive was very green and picturesque. One of the things I hate most about Australia, along with snakes and spiders, is the roads. You can be driving along a road, enjoying the scenery, when suddenly the road has turned in to a bridge spanning a huge gorge. You just look to your left and there's no ground at the side of you – just treetops or blue sky. Very scary but am getting used to it. Slowly.

SUNDAY 16 MARCH

Such a laugh this morning. Jasper Conran knocked on the husband's side of the bed, to ask him to get up and take him out to the toilet.

When the husband got up to put his robe on, Jasper jumped into his place and curled up on his pillow! He is a very clever dog. Husband is a very cross husband. Had a bit of a row with him tonight, actually. I mean the husband, not Jasper. He drove me to the Plaza, under protest, to buy emergency bread for girls' lunches tomorrow. I bought ricotta cheese, ham, garlic bread and chocolate, but forgot the bread for school lunches! You should have heard him whinge at me. I threw his wallet at him. Not speaking to him now.

Was reflecting today about what a simple life we're leading now, with regard to 'necessities.' In the UK I would have said that the telephone and internet were crucial to our well-being, as was cable tv and mobile phones. Also the Next Directory, Pet Plan Insurance and my subscription to Vogue magazine. You wouldn't believe how easy it is to manage without those items over here. (Admittedly though, work are paying for the internet subscription, so we're not completely cut off). Was aghast when I added up the cost of all the 'necessities' we're now managing without. It came to £203.00 per month. That's almost £2,500.00 per year. And when I logged-on to look back over the bank statements, you wouldn't believe how much money we spent in Sainsbury – it was just obscene. Our food bill here is at least half of what it was back home. Feeling very cross with self for not being a thriftier housewife much, much sooner. Still, better late than never.

WEEK 11
Crocodile is the New Cashmere

MONDAY 17 MARCH

Yes, yes, yes! Have lost a stone. Am overjoyed. Am becoming more ladylike every day. Going out walking now, and then going to make final decision on my new uniform.

Just been round the Oval with Jasper Conran. Some days our power walk slows to a crawl because so many people want to talk to him. I usually try to avoid the school-run time because that's when all the children stop to pat him.

Just been on the Hermes and Tods websites. Very frustrating because they were very slow and won't let you copy the images. Anyway, here is the list:

Tods: Calf leather wallet with alligator coin purse in either light sapphire or powder pink. Leather cuff in pale pink. Hand-braided bracelet in pale pink and topaz. Lizard print tote bag. Can't decide whether to go for their ballerina flats or sick with their traditional loafers. Will decide later.

Hermes: Osiris bracelet. Cape Cod watch. Kelly handbag. Conveniently, Hermes has three boutiques in Australia (Melbourne, Sydney and Gold Coast) so when we win the lottery I won't have far to go!

TUESDAY 18 MARCH

Terrible day, for a number of reasons. Firstly, we've been given notice by the letting agent that we cannot renew the lease on this house, so we have got to move out by the end of May. Is very stressful having to find another house, but probably just as well. This house is costing an arm and a leg and we're not using half the space we're paying for. We're hoping to get a one-storey for $400 per week. We'll start looking at the weekend. The agent is bringing round a potential buyer in the morning, so have got to clean and tidy as soon as family leave for work and school.

Secondly, had a bad fright when I went to dustbin this morning to find it full of wriggly maggots! They were crawling round the edge when I lifted the lid up and I had an absolute fit. Annie kindly gave us a lecture on how all bacteria is a living organism so it has the potential to turn into the little wrigglers.

Thirdly, think I need a hip replacement. Coupled with my poorly coccyx, I'm in a bad way and can't stand up. The pain makes me almost black out. Really ought to go to doctor. Will have to go soon as need more thyroxine, so will sort it asap.

Spent afternoon on internet and watched Heather Mills' rant outside the courtroom after the divorce settlement. Thought she was rather bitter for someone who'd just been given 20-odd million. Feel sure I'd have been much happier with that result! Wish my husband was worth a bit more. What do I get for being married almost 19 years? Whisked off to live with the snakes and spiders, that's what!

Speaking of snakes, there's an article in today's Macarthur Chronicle about a red-bellied black snake which was found lying in wait in the women's toilets at a leisure centre near us! Apparently, it had been seen staking out the centre for a few days, before it plucked up the courage to venture inside. Thank goodness it didn't decide to go to the gym in Narellan instead, as that's where the girls go on Sport Tuesdays.

WEDNESDAY 19 MARCH

For the first time in my life, I am in the right place at the right time. According to Harpers Bazaar, "crocodile is the new cashmere!" Wonder if meagre housekeeping budget can stretch to a new handbag? Will think very carefully about where any possible economies might be made.

THURSDAY 20 MARCH

Crocodile handbag will have to wait. Cannot even stretch to a tiny coin purse. Is not possible to make any more economies. Resorted to cutting own fringe today. Very scary but turned out ok. Lack of funds also caused me to rethink my new signature style uniform. Will never be able to afford Tods or Hermes unless the husband sells a few billion Gripples, so have downscaled my wishlist to Hobbs. Will probably be down to Primark next week.

Speaking of lack of funds, we had the bailiffs knocking at the door this morning. I thought they were chasing the previous tenants, as we receive lots of final demands in their name, but they were actually chasing the owner of the house – our landlord. It would appear that he's not paying the mortgage and is ignoring the letters from the bank. The house is being repossessed and we need to find new accommodation quickly.

After shock of dealing with bailiff, took myself off to Camden to calm down . Enjoyed smoked salmon sandwich in Gourmet Deli, then a wander around the town. Joined the library and went to Camden Council offices to register Jasper Conran and his microchip number. Annie had stayed late at school to edit a PE project, so we picked her up and called for a KFC and a drive through the countryside. On a hot day it's so nice to drive out in the air-conditioned truck. Returned home to torrential rain and thunderstorm. Lightening was very scary.

FRIDAY 21 MARCH

Not much to report today. Quietest Good Friday we've ever spent. Annie went to cinema and Lulu did her homework (!) Afraid I had another lost the plot day with regard to my diet – well it is Easter, isn't it. I decided to take a day off (from doing nothing) and sat on the balcony all afternoon, reading my library book and eating chocolate. Heavenly. Will make up for it later.

SATURDAY 22 MARCH

It looks like this house is going to be sold from under us, as last week's viewer returned today with her husband and son. They've just moved here from Queensland and the son is in Lulu's year at school. (Lulu is terribly perturbed that he's had a good look around her bedroom and seen all her stuff!) We desperately need a cheaper place, but I will miss my beloved balcony – it has become my own private haven these last few months.

SUNDAY 23 MARCH

I know that a troglodyte is someone who lives in a cave, but I wonder if there's a name for a person who lives on a balcony – other than 'loner' as my children like to call me. I went out there this morning to read for a few hours, had Annie supply me with toast mid-afternoon, spent a few hours sewing and then had pizza for dinner out there! Have only just come inside as it's now too dark to see. We do have a light, but it attracts too many buzzy, flying things. Think that moving out of this house will be a good thing if it forces me to interact with people more – have become too fond of my own company.

WEEK 12
Pots and Kettles

MONDAY 24 MARCH

Am in a bad way. Left hip has collapsed. Am in agony. Too ill to type.

TUESDAY 25 MARCH

Think it's a trapped nerve, so hopefully won't need plastic hip joint just yet. Still in blinding pain and unable to sit down.

WEDNESDAY 26 MARCH

Something rather wonderful has happened. Is quite a miracle. Has never happened to me before in 43 years – I HAVE LOST MY APPETITE! Must be the pain in my leg. Am wasting away. Can only lie on my bed, wracked with pain, reading a Penny Vincenzi blockbuster (is very good, all about the Lloyds scandal of the late 1980s). Was hoping I looked a bit pale and consumptive, but actually look quite hale and hearty. In fact, robust would probably be the best word to describe me – not really the delicate, ladylike look I was hoping for. Still, it's only been one day. Let's hope appetite doesn't return any time soon.

THURSDAY 27 MARCH

Oh no! Nigella is here in Sydney. Hope she hasn't come to get me for being bitchy. Think she must have read what I wrote about being thinner than her, because apparently she's hired a personal trainer. She will definitely be thinner than me now. On the subject of Nigella though, have to say that she has a very successful, if rather boring, personal uniform. She always wears stretchy, long black dresses with brightly coloured cashmere cardigans or denim jackets. Last year she wrote an article in American Harpers about it. Was very interesting. Oh, I absolutely MUST get back into my fitness regime. Leg is still very painful, but once I get moving it calms down. The pain mainly occurs when I try to get up after sitting down – almost fainted this morning.

FRIDAY 28 MARCH

Have definitely learnt my lesson about gossiping and being catty, after the shock of thinking that Nigella had come over to tell me off, but I just have to ask – have you seen the photos of Pierce Brosnan's wife? I know this is pots and kettles, and they're both definitely black, but she is quite a large lady. There's a photo of her in a bikini on the front page of a gossipy weekly magazine. She is very brave, and very beautiful, and I do admire her for not hiding under a beach towel. Anyway, she has the last laugh, doesn't she – she goes to bed with Pierce every night. Daren't say any more, don't want 007 after me as well.

SATURDAY 29 MARCH

Leg is still agony and am living on max strength Cuprinol tablets (luckily, there are no calories in them). Cannot sit down to type, so no diary for a few days.

WEEK 13
Troubled Times

WEDNESDAY 2 APRIL

Am back, but still in agony. Have been to see doctor today, and she's sending me for a CT scan on leg and coccyx. She thinks it's a trapped nerve. However, this creates yet more problems because if the CT scanner is fully enclosed, I won't be able to do it due to severe claustrophobia (remember the tunnels?)

Doctor also issued prescription for thyroxine, and this was equally troubling. Both doctor, nurse and pharmacist gave precise instructions about keeping thyroxine tablets in the fridge at a very specific temperature, and were absolutely amazed when I showed them my current tablets which are housed in a blister pack. Is all a bit worrying. Am also troubled because I've always kept a very close and informed eye upon my treatment and thyroxine levels etc. and over here the scale and parameters are totally different, so I have absolutely no idea what the readings mean. I feel terribly out-of-control with it all. I had a blood test and have to go back to doc next week.

Anyway, despite severe leg pain, we have still been on trips out and about in New South Wales. Husband just has to stop the truck every half an hour for me to get out and change position. Last week we went to Woy Woy, which is north of Sydney on the Central Coast. The road was cut out of the mountain, but the rock in the middle of the road, between the two lanes, had been left in place. Woy Woy is very picturesque. It's built on a huge inlet and is very lush and green. All the houses have their own mooring for their yachts and motor boats.

Apart from a few trips out, I've been mostly confined to my balcony. When not sewing or reading, I spend my time worrying – mostly about the UK house and the lack of sale in the depressed UK housing market, about whether to rent the house out, about paying solicitor for Power of Attorney which we didn't actually need as there has been no sale, about having to move out of this rental house as it has been sold, about finding another house to rent, preferably a much cheaper one, about whether a much cheaper one will be very grotty, about money, about girls; the list is endless. If only I could get paid for worrying, I'd earn a fortune.

FRIDAY 4 APRIL

Cannot walk. Too poorly and depressed to type.

SATURDAY 5 APRIL

Things are very fraught here in Harrington Park. Tempers in the Young household are frayed to their absolute limits. It all centres around the UK housing market. Our house still has no buyer, despite huge price reduction. We have now realised that we just cannot afford to sell. We will be throwing away our equity. We have very reluctantly instructed the estate agent to rent the house out. I am very much against this but have no choice. We're still paying the mortgage and insurance, and in another couple of months we also have to pay half-price council tax.

So, in order to accommodate all this expense we need to move to a much cheaper house over here. Went to view a one-storey this morning which was much, much cheaper but was also much, much smaller. You should have heard the howls of protest from the family. Anybody would think I was asking them to live in a tent, not just downsize for a while.

SUNDAY 6 APRIL

Have decided to forgive unsupportive family for their criticism of my housing plans. Have made my views plain to husband and told him he should lease the teeny tiny one-storey (will be in his name as he is the wage-earner – I am persona non grata in Australia). Lulu says it will be the worst six months of her life. Annie is quite stoical about it, just worried about her drum kit which will have to be wrapped in blankets and stored in the garage. Anyway, have decided to leave it all in the husband's hands and let him handle it all. He and Lulu favour a townhouse in Camden, which is very nice but £370 per week – over a month this adds up to $280 more than the one-storey. Husband is going to call the agents about both properties tomorrow, so will see how he gets on.

We drove into Sydney today, and had another tour round the bays. Day started off with amusing incident, although husband might present a different opinion if he was writing this diary.

Girls and I had showers, did hair and make-up etc. while husband prepared a delicious picnic – egg sandwiches, tuna, cheese and tomato, fresh orange juice, mini-pizza snacks, he really excelled himself.

However, girls and I were starving hungry after all the effort of getting ready, and somehow we accidentally ate the picnic while we were still parked in the drive and the husband was busy consulting his map book and programming the SatNav! He was very cross with us, but we did save him a sandwich.

Had to drive through tunnels on way to Double Bay, which was obviously an ordeal for me, but totally worth it. The bay was every bit as glamorous as it seemed last time. Kept an eye out for Nicole, as she was spotted having lunch in Sydney yesterday with Naomi Watts, but didn't see her anywhere.

Went back to the lovely stationery shop in the chic arcade, but it was closed – much to my dismay and the husband's relief. Enjoyed cornettos and diet coke on a bench in a little park. Had to hide Jasper Conran under the bench as dogs were not allowed. Luckily, he was very quiet for a change, but just as I was boasting about what a well-behaved dog he was, I realised he was actually chewing some gum he'd found under the bench! Girls disgusted with him.

WEEK 14
Chubby Laurels

MONDAY 7 APRIL

Whoever would believe that we've been here 13 weeks already? Girls are ready for a break from school, they are exhausted. They have exams this week ("half-yearlies") and then break-up on Friday afternoon for two weeks. Upon returning to school, they will have to change over into 'winter uniform.' This consists of a green tartan tabard and white blouse! They didn't protest as much as I expected when they went for the fitting appointment – I think they're just resigned to the frumpy uniform now.

My CT scan has finally been booked. Am going to the clinic at Campbelltown on Wednesday afternoon at 3.00pm. Apparently, the machine is a 'do-nut' scanner and is not enclosed, which means my claustrophobia will not be a problem.

Went to view the townhouse in Camden tonight. However the landlord had changed the locks (suspect the last tenant was a bad one) and the agent could not gain entry. On paper at least, it would appear we can afford up to $370 rental per week and still pay the bills back home. If we manage to get a tenant in our house, we will have no worries at all. Still can't believe the market could fall so dramatically just when we need to sell-up.

TUESDAY 8 APRIL

I have no news today. Leg is so bad that I stayed in bed until 2.00pm, when I forced myself to get up and make dinner for girls. Had to sit on top step for 10 mins to recover from pain of standing up. Was worried I might faint and fall upon poor little Jasper Conran, squashing him to death. I made him sit on the top step until I was safely on the bottom.

WEDNESDAY 9 APRIL

Finally know what's wrong with my back/leg, but don't really understand what it means until I see the doctor tomorrow. I have a "large central and left-sided L5/S1 disc protrusion indenting the thecal sac and extending into the left lateral recess of S1 where it is compressing the left S1 nerve root." I only know all this because I opened the x-ray pictures and report which I have to hand to the doctor. Feeling very worried. She left message on husband's mobile for me to ring her and make appointment re recent blood tests, so think there could also be something amiss there.

Scan was hideous, but only because I am such a wimp. It was very open and the tunnel part was very short. Clinic was quite funny. Receptionist was called Marge and had a very broad Australian accent. Felt as if I was in an episode of Neighbours! Marge was very kind and not at all cross with me for forgetting to take my Medicare card with me. She just rang up their central office to get my number. System is very efficient.

THURSDAY 10 APRIL

It was not good news at the doctor. Apparently, my cholesterol and blood sugar levels are both raised. Can't think why they should be, as have been more active and eaten much more healthily than did back home. Thyroid levels were stable, thank goodness. Have been given eating plan and need to refine diet. Need to eat more wholegrains. Am switching entire family onto wholemeal bread immediately, and will have cereal for breakfast and supper.

Regarding my back, news was even worse. The lower disc is bulging so badly it's pressing on the main nerve. If it gets any worse, I can expect to lose bowel and bladder control and lose all feeling in left leg. That would mean emergency surgery. However, am sure that will not happen. The other possibility is that the anti-inflammatory tablets will reduce the inflammation enough to shrink the disc away from the nerve and therefore eliminate the leg pain. This would then be a case of simply making sure the disc did not deteriorate further, by being careful not to lift or bend. This is the option I'm going for. Doctor is sending me to see a neurosurgeon for an expert opinion on the position of the disc, and I have to make appointment tomorrow. Don't know whether Medicare covers cost of neurosurgeon or operation. Husband will have to ring Medicare and clarify position. Have taken anti-inflammatory tablets and feel better already.

Doctor kept asking me if I'd had an accident recently, which would account for the sudden deterioration in my back. I kept saying no, but then suddenly on way home I remembered – I did have an accident. It must be damaged from when I fell down the bank and nearly landed in the creek when I was rescuing the lost dog. That little mutt has a lot to answer for. Is going to prove a very costly rescue attempt.

The husband has had a very good day today, and taken another big order. He's enjoying his job very much and meets some interesting people. He met someone from Manchester today, who told him we should be living on the Northern Beach (yes, we know we should) and who offered to build us a lovely house for $100k – I've told the husband to keep in touch with him!

FRIDAY 11 APRIL

Took my new medication last night and woke up this morning almost pain-free for the first time in three weeks. Is a minor miracle. Obviously, the disc is still damaged, that won't just correct itself, but the inflammation must have subsided enough to free the nerve and therefore stop causing me such agony. Feel so relieved. Appointment with neurosurgeon is a week on Wednesday.

SATURDAY 12 APRIL

Husband and I abandoned girls and dog and went off for a romantic coastal jaunt by ourselves. We walked along the beach at Dee Why holding hands. Had a lovely time. Enjoyed a cool drink at sea-front bar and watched the surfers for an hour.

During the drive to Dee Why, we were listening to the radio and they were covering the 'Wife Carrying Championships!' Husband heaved a sigh of relief that he didn't have to enter. It was so ludicrous that I turned it off before the end of the race. The whole thing descended into madness for me when they kept talking about 'George the Boilerman' and asking competitors which position gave them the best chance of completing the course! (Apparently, it's dangling the wife across your back, with her legs over your shoulders).

SUNDAY 13 APRIL

Disastrous day. Can barely walk, so therefore no fitness routine. Healthy eating regime not well-received by ungrateful family. They are unimpressed with rye bread, proclaiming it too tough, and refused to eat brown rice with last night's beef stroganoff. Gave them lecture on good fats v bad fats (gleaned from cholesterol information leaflet handed out by doctor) but to no avail. Afraid healthy eating message was seriously compromised by proclaiming self too ill to cook and therefore sending husband out for KFC at dinnertime. Really must capitalise on stone lost so far, instead of resting on chubby laurels. Will begin tomorrow.

WEEK 15
Eviction Notice

MONDAY 14 APRIL

Am very worried. Have been bitten on right foot. Why does it always happen to me? Have no idea when or where it happened, but it's agony. Foot is itching off and you can track the line of poison inching its way along the vein. It hasn't got very far yet though, so I presume it's nothing to worry about. I suggested to the husband that he try sucking the poison out, but he was not enthusiastic. Have told him he'll feel very guilty if I don't wake up tomorrow.

Very quiet first day of school holidays. Make a scrumptious dinner tonight, using new recipe in Annabel Karmel cookery book. It involved onion, mushroom, chicken, bacon, cream and pasta. I know the cream shouldn't have been in there, but will use crème fraiche in future. Am making conscientious effort to eat more fruit, so had an apple and two oranges today. My appetite is still very poor, but sadly this is not being reflected by any drop in weight. Will be relieved when neurosurgeon appointment is over with. Am clinging to hope that some sort of physiotherapy will sort me out. If I need an operation, I'm jumping off the Harbour Bridge!

TUESDAY 15 APRIL

What a relief. Woke up this morning safe and sound. Angry bite has turned into a dull bruise and the poison is retreating back down the vein and fading rapidly. Obviously, my fit little anti-bodies have successfully repelled the invaders. If only the disc in my back would stir itself into similar action.

I still think a more loving husband would not have hesitated to suck the poison out immediately, rather than leaving anti-bodies to fight it out overnight. What if they'd failed? He'd have spent the rest of his life wishing he'd stuck my foot in his mouth.

WEDNESDAY 16 APRIL

My tolerance threshold for living with the horrors of Australia increases daily, much to my surprise. This morning I found a huge redback on the patio, and my adrenaline meter barely flinched. I simply strolled back into the house to collect my can of Mortein and blasted it into oblivion. Am studiously ignoring the fact that it may have been living in the cavity wall, and also the fact that it may have been co-habiting with web-mates or relations.

THURSDAY 17 APRIL

Opened the door this afternoon to find the friendly bailiff had returned, and he kindly served me with an Eviction Notice – the house we are living in has been repossessed by the bank, and we have to vacate it within 28 days! It would be fair to say the Australian Experience is not running quite as smoothly as planned.

On a lighter note, husband, Lulu and I went to the launch party tonight of a new gated community of houses within Harrington Park. There were about 25 houses within the compound and they shared a swimming pool, spa, tennis court, BBQ area and pavilion. It was all very luxurious. We had wine and canapes and pretended to be seriously interested in buying a house. Didn't have the heart to tell the builder that we're stuck in the mad property market back home and haven't got a hope in hell of selling anything at the moment. Things can only get better. At least for the husband, who is jetting off to Melbourne for 2 days.

SATURDAY 19 APRIL

My glamorous new life is going awry. The trapped-nerve pain in my leg has returned and all I have done for two days is lie in bed and read. The husband arrived home from Melbourne (tired and hungover) after lunch and took Jasper and I out to Camden for a stroll up and down Argyle Street. Husband and Jasper strolled, I limped. Enjoyed half an hour in the bookshop while the boys rested on a seat in the sunshine. Found two good books and will drop heavy hints to girls as Mothers' Day is finally celebrated here next month. The first book was "How Not to Look Old," and the second one was "From Frumpy to Foxy in 15 Minutes." Think my need for the first one is greatest, as it would be preferable to look younger and frumpy than to look old and foxy.

SUNDAY 20 APRIL

My nerves are in shreds. Went out for nice peaceful Sunday afternoon drive and the husband scared me to death. First he announced we were going to drive "over the flood plains, where all the water runs into the township," and then announced that we had to drive through "Death Valley" to get there. Sometimes, his little jokes wear a bit thin. He'd just stopped chuckling at the look on my face when we passed a sign proclaiming we were in a "Wildlife Corridor" and to beware of Kangaroos and Koalas for the next 20km. Luckily, it also mentioned that the peak time for encountering them was between dusk and dawn, so it appeared we were safe.

My heartbeat had just returned to normal after first spotting the sign, when the husband decided to recount a little tale he heard during the Melbourne trip. The car service sent the same driver as last time, a lady called "Linda" apparently. They were discussing kangaroos, as you do in Australia, and the likelihood of hitting one on the roads. Whereas previously I thought the worst that could happen to you was if one landed through your windscreen and squashed you to death, Linda informed him that it's also possible for them to land through your windscreen and rip you to shreds with their razor-sharp talons. I'd heard on wildlife programmes how when kangaroo males are fighting, they can disembowel each other with their claws, so you can imagine the mincemeat they'd make of two little humans strapped in their car seats.

Spent the return journey planning our move to a chic harbour-side apartment, before returning to earth and remembering our plight re UK housing market. Never mind. Will instead instigate a curfew that truck must be in drive and all members of family must be in house by dusk. That should keep us all safe from any marauding wildlife. (Must also remember to instruct secretary to book a different car service next time husband goes to Melbourne – think we've had quite enough of "Linda's" cautionary tales).

WEEK 16
Life is a Trial

MONDAY 21 APRIL

The husband is definitely banned from any more jetsetting to Melbourne. Was in car tonight when he accidentally played an old voicemail message on his mobile. It was from the boss and said, "G'day Mate, just ringing to check that you're still alive. Your 'plane leaves at 10.30am." Strongly suspect that far more alcohol is consumed on these trips than have previously supposed. Hhmmm …

Husband finished work at 4.00pm tonight so we could drive round the estate agents and attempt to find somewhere to live. The tiny one-storey is long gone, much to relief of spoilt family. Only one possible rental fitted the bill, so we drove down to look at it. Sounded ideal on paper. Address was same as a very nice development we saw last week, so we presumed it was one of the lovely new houses. However, SatNav took us way past the new estate, down the lane and directed us to a house at the bottom. Was a hideous little shack, overgrown and neglected. Next door neighbours were in front garden in their matching tracksuits. She had bleached blonde hair in a high ponytail and was smoking. Could only see bottom half of his tracksuit as he was half hidden under the bonnet of a car. She stared at us as we slowed down, but we pretended not to look and just kept on going! Hope we have more luck tomorrow.

Am beginning to seriously worry. We have to leave this house in 23 days. Still have not sorted out the rental of our house in UK. Major article on the news tonight about the Australian dollar being very strong. This means that even if we managed to sell our house, it's not a good time to exchange any money, and the exchange rate is already 20% down on what it was last summer when we did our calculations. I didn't expect life here to be a piece of cake, but I could just do with only having to cope with one problem at once. At the moment we're coping with a) being stuck in the madly crashing property market at home, b) being served with eviction notice, c) rising rental costs here, d) exchange rate working against us and finally, e) my leg/trapped nerve/bulging disc problem. Life is a trial.

TUESDAY 22 APRIL

Could not sleep last night. Am in state of total panic. Bird flu has reared it's ugly head on my list of urgent issues to worry about. In fact, it's even overtaken the "Finding Somewhere to Live Before We're Evicted" issue. Read on internet that Japan is going to immunise 10 million key people against a likely pandemic. They wouldn't do that if they didn't think it was necessary, would they? Lay awake all night making plans to quarantine family in event of global outbreak. Looks like I'll be stockpiling tins of Aldi rice pudding and tomato soup in garage.

Calmed down slightly when I remembered that the Olympic Games are being held in Beijing this year, which is much nearer the epicentre than I am. Millions of people will be involved with that and they wouldn't all be planning to go if they were likely to be struck down, would they? WOULD THEY?

WEDNESDAY 23 APRIL

Has been a day of good news and bad news.

Firstly, husband and I went to view a one-storey house this morning. It is perfectly adequate, but obviously not on the grand scale of this one. It has four bedrooms so the husband can still have an office, and all the bedrooms have built-in wardrobes so we don't need to worry about furniture. Was ecstatic to find that it has two loos, as it only mentioned one in the brochure. The shower room can be accessed from the main bedroom and also from the hall, so that could make for some interesting surprises in the mornings if anyone forgets to lock the relevant doors! I will miss my balcony. Not looking forward to being back on the ground. There were about six couples viewing the house, and all applied to rent it. Husband went down to the Plaza to hand in our application form and schmoozed the agent for five minutes. She rang back an hour later to say that we'd got it. It's a huge relief to know that we're sorted for the next 12 months. Lulu is not amused at having to downsize her bedroom, but it's still larger than her old one back home, so I'm standing no nonsense from her!

Went to see neurosurgeon this afternoon. Is not good news. She is almost certain that I will need an operation. A few years ago I had a split disc and all the acid leaked out. From what I can gather (she is Eastern European and difficult to understand) it is this acid which has calcified and caused the bulge which is now pressing on the nerve. She needs to go in with her scalpel and scrape away the build-up in order to free the nerve. However, to be sure of this, she needs to see an MRI scan. My heart immediately started racing and I told her that I wouldn't be able to do it, due to severe claustrophobia. She replied that I could be sedated, and gave me a form to take to the radiographer and arrange an appointment. Have to go back and see her again with the results, then she'll make a decision.

Paid the bill and returned to truck in floods of tears. Poor husband was bewildered. Basically, I would rather face 20 operations than one MRI scan. He made me go to radiographer and arrange appointment. He couldn't go in with me because there was nowhere to park. I was wiping tears away as I spoke to receptionist, so she clearly thought I was an insane person. However, it turns out that I am not the only insane person to enter their building because the waiting list for sedation is very long. A nurse came out and tried to talk me into trying the scan without sedation, as I could have an immediate appointment for that. I flatly refused. She obviously thought I was a complete wimp and said they'd ring me with an appointment date next week, but it would be at least June before one is available. Suits me. The longer away the better. Am in state of total terror.

Neurologist gave me some strong painkillers but warned they will make me drowsy, and am only allowed one per day. As I unpacked my bag and put the pills in the kitchen, the mother in me automatically warned girls they mustn't touch my tablets as they're very dangerous. They scoffed at me and asked if I thought they were aged 3 and 4. The naughty girls then kept taking it turns to touch the tablets and fall on the floor, pretending to die! Teenagers are very sarcastic animals.

Went to bed very depressed. Tried to look on the bright side, but only positive thought was that at least I won't be a homeless invalid. Is surely better to have roof over useless body than to be cast out on the streets.

THURSDAY 24 APRIL

Took new painkiller last night and had best night's sleep for weeks. Got up today in optimistic mood. Had yet another stern talk with self and decided to put on a brave face and make a more determined effort to look on the bright side. Do not want girls to be worried and affected by my ailments, so it's important that I rise above it all. Actually, not much chance of girls being worried and affected, considering that they limp around making fun of me and telling me to "shake a leg." Heartless beasts.

Have let everything slide in last four weeks of illness. My self-improvement programme has gone to the dogs. My diet plan has flown out of the window. My exercise routine has died an early death. Need to get life back on track, so began by going to the mall for the afternoon. Had a lovely time, although didn't look very chic. Was horrified to see reflection in large shop mirror in David Jones. Is very disheartening to find self back at Square One, but I refuse to be beaten by a dodgy disc and a rogue nerve. Will begin my transformation again. Will start tomorrow.

FRIDAY 25 APRIL

Is no good. Brave faces and Bright Sides have not worked. Am a broken woman. Will my poor body ever be mended?

SUNDAY 27 APRIL

No news to report. I look very wretched. My Wallis Simpson furrowed brow is almost split in half with pain, and I look pale and sickly. Hope tomorrow is a better day.

PART TWO
The Doll's House

WEEK 17
It's a Dog's Life

MONDAY 28 APRIL

Girls went back to school today. Got up with them and took my Tramadol tablet, then laid down again for 5 minutes. Next thing I knew, it was 13.08pm. Must not let this happen tomorrow. Walked Jasper Conran round the block, and endured very tricky moment when he needed a poopy. Am in too much pain to bend down and scoop it up with my plastic bag, so I have to actually get down on my knees, do the necessary and then struggle to my feet again. Whole process takes so long, and I spend so much time on my knees, that I'm sure I look like I'm religiously worshipping the poo! Poor old Harrington Park just didn't know what hit it when I arrived to live here!

TUESDAY 29 APRIL

I can't believe it. Just our rotten luck. There are two huge houses on the rental market and one of them is only $10 per week more than the one we've chosen. We haven't signed the lease yet, so we could give backword, but I just haven't got the energy to go through the selection process again. Waiting to see if you've been successful is really nerve-wracking, and we can't risk any rejections consider-ing we're under notice of eviction. Still really cross though. One of them has a massive covered balcony which stretches right across the front of the house. Jasper and I could have LIVED on there!

WEDNESDAY 30 APRIL

Visit to real estate agent this morning to sign new rental agreement. Agent made a mistake though. We asked for a 12 month lease, and she gave us a 6 month one. We didn't correct her. After seeing the huge houses on rental market this week, and the slight decrease in rental prices, we've decided the shorter lease suits us better. Major problem with Jasper Conran though – he must not be allowed in the house under any circumstances! Lovely agent smiled and talked about 'turning a blind eye.' She warned us that the landlady lives around the corner though, and that we must be careful. This means that the neighbours are probably her friends, and could be spying on us! Will have to be very careful.

Felt a bit down when we looked around the new house tonight. It's a far cry from the luxury we've become used to. How will we manage without an en-suite and walk-in wardrobe? At least everywhere was relatively clean, if rather shabby. Some of the blinds are broken and one lounge window has no blind at all, but I can soon make a voile to hang up. Am very much looking forward to cheering the place up, and will start by making new cushions and throws for the sofas. The agent forgot to ask the landlady if we were allowed to paint the girls' bedrooms, so we're still waiting for an answer on that.

Annie was in disgrace tonight. Instead of coming straight home after school, she sent a text informing me that she was at the Plaza with her friends. Sent one back saying that dinner was ready and to get herself home immediately. She still hadn't appeared an hour later. She finally turned up with her friend Hannah and a stray dog in tow! I was not pleased. Hannah's mum appeared and took the dog to the vet for its microchip reading, and vet then rang the owner who turned up at the surgery to collect it. Have had enough stray dog sagas on Harrington Park and do not wish for any more. Still, at least the stray dogs get more excitement than I do at the moment.

THURSDAY 1 MAY

Moving day got off to a bad start when Jasper Conran cocked his leg and peed all over Annie's school bag in the hallway. Couldn't work out why he'd done it, until I picked up the bag to clean it and found it was covered in stray dog hairs, hence Jasper making his mark. Cleaned it hurriedly and packed Annie off to school – am still not amused by the stray dog saga. Lulu stayed off school today to help with the move. An extra pair of hands was invaluable, seeing as I'm unable to lift anything and can barely walk. The boss's father also came along with his pick-up truck to help the husband with the washing machine, fridge and beds – he is very kind. When Neil left, husband and I went to the pet shop and bought a 'doggy play-pen' and made Jasper Conran a comfortable little compound in the garden, beneath the sheltered pergola. He was not happy though, and cried and screamed all afternoon. Eventually had to go round to the neighbours and apologise for the noise. Moved him into the garage, but that just made an even worse racket due to the echo from the large ill-fitting metal door. He could be heard right down the end of the cul-de-sac. Other dogs from neighbouring streets were joining in – it was like a scene from 101 Dalmations!

Sent husband out for pizza at 5.30pm, as far too busy to cook. Is now 10.30pm and almost sorted. Had a call from agent to say the landlady is happy for us to paint whatever we want, providing we don't use outlandish colours.

Everybody quite comfortable, although still feel house is very shabby compared to what we have been used to. However, have to keep reminding self that we're saving $130 per week, and that's a lot of money. Spent a pleasant half-hour daydreaming about what I could buy with that money if it wasn't being used to pay bills. Top of the list was haircut/colour, then Clarins Beauty Flash Balm followed by manicure and leg wax. Hope I don't forget myself one day and stumble into the Plaza's beauty salon by mistake. Would be a financial disaster. But if my head was a bit wuzzy from my very strong painkillers, it would not be my fault if I didn't know what I was doing. Would it? Will keep you informed.

FRIDAY 2 MAY

Am feeling under siege. Is like living with the threat of a sniper's bullet. Am convinced landlady is spying on us from behind the neighbour's fence, so everytime Jasper Conran goes near a window, we have to throw ourselves in front of him, bodyguard style. He's very perturbed, and quite afraid of being squashed to death. Think he'd prefer being thrown on the streets for breaking Tenancy Agreement to sudden death at such a tender age. He didn't settle very well last night, and had me up at 2.00am, 4.00am and 6.00am. Didn't need toilet, just wanted to nosey around the garden. Discovered a small herb bed with a chilli plant and was so cross at lack of sleep, was tempted to let him lick it. Overcame ill-will and pulled him away just in time!

New house is very cold in the mornings. Husband grumbles it doesn't help that I won't allow blinds to be opened to let in the sunshine, in case neighbours spot Mr Conran skipping around the house. I've told them all to put an extra jumper on. JC's welfare is far more important than those three feeling a little chilly. It's all about priorities.

Being in new house has resurrected that holiday feeling (girls actually said it's like living in a shabby holiday let, but am ignoring that comment). Sent husband out for alcohol and takeaways. Am just not a drinker these days, so did not know what to request. He did well though, and brought back beer (for himself) and a tasty, light, raspberry-flavoured wine called Sparkletini for me. Had a nice evening watching tv (husband, girls and Jasper) and reading magazines (me). Think we'll be ok in this house. Our bank balance certainly will.

SATURDAY 3 MAY

Oh what a day – haven't enjoyed myself so much for ages. Have been on a little spending spree, and realised how much I've missed the mall. Need to brighten up the Doll's House, but only on a tiny little budget so had to choose purchases very carefully.

In Vogue Living there's a regular advert for an American interior design company called Nancy Corzine, and the photos in these ads always inspire me. After studying them carefully last night, I set off to Campbelltown this morning fired with enthusiasm to choose material and sparkly, gorgeous, trinkets to turn the Dolls House into a chic haven of good taste.

Faltered slightly at the first hurdle, but recovered quite well. The budget warehouse-type store sells lots of cheap material, but no NICE cheap material. However, had just lost hope among the rolls of fluorescent fleece and polyester florals, when I spotted a small stand of Indian cottons, marked with a 20% discount. Bought 2.5m in green, and 6 cushion inners. Material only came to $19 and cushions to $18. Also saw a sage green rug for $70, but undecided about this. We desperately need a rug, but the ones I like are all very expensive. $70 very reasonable, but not sure about the colour. The thrifty housewife in me decided to consider it carefully for a few days. Long gone are the days when I would make rash purchases which would hide in my wardrobe and only see the light of day on their way to the dustbin.

After the warehouse I hit the Mall – my favourite place. Went to 'Hot Dollar' and bought some small trays and a basket in lime green, to organise our toothbrushes and make-up on the vanity unit. Now that there are so many of us getting ready in the same place, it gets a bit messy (especially when teenagers are incapable of tidying up after themselves!) Trays and basket were only $2 each.

Headed to Lincraft next, a huge material/craft store. Bought some larger cushion inners and 2.5m of black cord material – very chic.

Finally went to 'House' – a lovely homewares store. Could not resist some very sophisticated green wine glasses – in the sale at $12.95 for a set of four. Also bought two large silver place mats to put on the breakfast bar in front of the high stools. Spotted lots of lovely ornaments, plant pots, china etc. but resisted. Have discovered iron willpower, and not before time.

Was just walking through mall to meet husband in car park, when was accosted by Annie. She was going to the cinema with

Hannah and needed money – it didn't take that girl long to find her feet!

Yet another quiet evening. Sat out on terrace with a magazine and a large cold drink. I miss my balcony very much but needs must, and my cloth has been cut accordingly.

SUNDAY 4 MAY

Oh how the Gods much chuckle when they're dealing with me. Feel sure they sit there in the heavens, up on their cloud, dreaming of ways to torment me to the limits of my endurance. Woke up this morning covered in huge, painful red blotches. It would appear that the insects had me for supper while I sat on the terrace last night. This never happened on my beloved balcony. Looked in mirror and heart sank to boots again. The Gods use me as their personal version of snakes and ladders. They let me advance 3 places and then push me backwards 4 or 5. They let my skin clear up, see me lose a stone and cut my hair successfully, but then they give me a bulging disc, a trapped nerve, leave me practically housebound and then cover me in huge red insect bites. Well, I'll show them. I won't be defeated. Time to regroup and start again. Again.

(Good news though, is that I'm feeling a little more relaxed about the whole Jasper Conran/indoor dog ban situation. Have devised system of black sheet pinned up at patio door, which means it's not possible for anyone to see inside and catch a glimpse of Mr Conran reclining on my sofas, with his delicate little head resting on my decorative cushions).

WEEK 18
Innocent as a Rose

MONDAY 5 MAY

Am very excited. Husband (being such a good husband) is very concerned about my damaged back/nerve and is very keen to cheer me up. He keeps mentioning Mother's Day (which is on Sunday) and I get the feeling that the world could be my oyster. A very small oyster, obviously, and probably one that's not all that fresh, possibly on the point of developing food-poisoning bugs, but still, an oyster all the same. Need to think very carefully about what I might like.

Have just been round the lake with Jasper Conran. We are only 5 minutes' walk from the lake and Plaza now, and it's so convenient. Met a friendly old man on my walk, who regaled me with tales about bushfires and how, as a young boy, he had to haul sacks of sand up the mountains to help extinquish the fires. He said we've been very lucky this year as the mild summer meant we've escaped the fires for once. Made me a bit nervous, to be honest, but I'm not going to dwell on it. My Worry List is full and I suspect there won't be vacancy until my scan is over and done with. Also met a woman who told me I should throw Jasper Conran in the lake to cure his fear of water (she had watched me carry him over the bridge). I did not stop to chat with her.

Caught up on all the washing, ironing etc. so that next two days are clear for Mr Conran and I to do some sewing.

WEDNESDAY 7 MAY

Jasper and I have been very busy. We've transformed the Ikea sofas with some very sophisticated cushions. Need to purchase another two seater now, as we're all very squashed when we sit down to watch tv together.

The Dolls House is looking much improved, despite the fact that the husband appears to have lost his initial willingness to paint the walls. Have resolved not to nag. Nagging is counter-productive. Being quietly sad and disappointed works much better!

THURSDAY 8 MAY

A miracle has happened. I am getting better. The anti-inflammatories have obviously decided to work at last, and today I feel brilliant. Hope I can get my plans back on track now.

FRIDAY 9 MAY

We have all become used to our new lodgings. Girls know their way to and from the school bus stop, and find it's a much shorter trek than before. Jasper and I walk around the lake every morning and afternoon, and today we explored all the side streets and footpaths around Salter Place. It's only a two minute walk up to Four Seasons Park, and there in the middle of the green we found a pavilion just like the one in The Sound of Music, where Liesl and Rolf shelter from the rain! We were very excited. I wanted to jump up on the seats and leap around them, but the gap between the benches was far too wide for me – sadly, it needed someone with far more grace and agility than I possess. (Came away with head filled with plans to make a white organza dress, though!)

SATURDAY 10 MAY

Terrible day today. Everyone in cranky moods and snappy with each other. We have these days every now and again. Husband said he wished I'd never come over here, Lulu hates our family and I wish I'd stayed at home! Annie is the only one who keeps a level head, and she's the only one who didn't want to come here! It always blows over though, and today was no exception. Think the bad mood was brought on by tension over the recent internet debacle. We've run up yet another huge bill, and have had to ban girls from using the internet for the moment until we sign up for our own plan. We can't take advantage of the boss' generosity yet again. We're not being greedy, it's just that the system is so different to home and we didn't understand how it works. It would appear that it's the girls using MSN and webcams that's running up the bill. This means they can't communicate with their friends until we sort out our own plan, but this is easier said than done. Even after two hours in the store, and two visits back home for yet more documentation, we still haven't been able to sign up. It's all to do with not living here long enough. Husband has to get some more ID from the bank and then try again later.

SUNDAY 11 MAY

Had a great Mother's Day. Girls and Jasper gave me three cute cards and the dvd of "27 Dresses." Husband told us all to be ready for noon, (no easy feat now that we're down to only one bathroom) and think where we wanted to go. All agreed it would be nice to go to the chic stationery shop in Double Bay. Was a bit wary of subjecting my leg/coccyx to a long journey, but decided it was a risk worth taking. Trouble is, by the time we'd stopped off at KFC (husband and Lulu), Opporto Chicken (me and Annie), skilfully negotiated the gridlock on way into city (husband) and hyperventilated in the tunnels (me), it was almost 3.00pm and the stationery shop was closed! Gazed through window with nose pressed against glass, and husband declared what a shame it was closed, as he'd brought $50 for me to spend in there! Was very disappointed, but we stopped at the Chocolate Café instead and what an experience that was. We sat at an outside table, as we had Mr Conran with us, and ate the best chocolate I've ever tasted. We ordered chocolate orange drinks, chocolate waffle ball drinks, chocolate brownies, chocolate cookies with macadamia nuts and a sundae-type dish that consisted of melted chocolate mixed with praline, nuts and ice-cream, topped with tiny chocolate covered malt balls! It was out-of-this-world, and all for only $40. Must go there again, especially as all the waitresses admired Mr Conran.

On way home bought hot BBQ chicken, smoked salmon, fresh bread and Caesar salad for dinner. Was delicious . Had intended to sit down and watch 27 Dresses, but had too much to do. Girls had homework and I had to take up the hem on Lulu's winter school pinafore (she tried the re-modelling trick again, but I didn't fall for it). Early to bed tonight, as everyone has a very early start in the morning. Well, everyone except me and Jasper Conran!

WEEK 19
Limping Feet Have Got No Rhythm

MONDAY 12 MAY

Another day, another diet. Am now feeling quite desperate, and desperate times call for drastic measures. Have bought box of "Fat Blaster" meal replacement drinks. Will have nothing but chocolate milkshake for breakfast, lunch and dinner for the next seven days. Have completely gone off food. Girls actually accused me of being anorexic, as they say I never eat. I say they've obviously soon forgotten yesterday's blow-out at the Chocolate Café!

TUESDAY 13 MAY

Have become veritable martyr to my leg. Need to keep it limber, and so walk around the lake every morning and evening, and up to Liesl's pavilion at lunchtime. Daren't let up with exercise, even for a day, in case it seizes up again.

WEDNESDAY 14 MAY

Leg is still much improved, am very relieved to report, although am sad to say that sometimes I have a slight limp, which is obviously not a look I was aiming for. Feeling very edgy, as am terrified of doing anything at all to upset delicate balance of trapped nerve again. Have reluctantly shelved plans to try out the Ingleburn Swing Dance Group. Must try looking on the Bright Side again, but be more persistent this time. Will begin tomorrow.

THURSDAY 15 MAY

Quiet day. Have finally started my chocolate milkshake diet. Was held up by not having the correct equipment. You need a special shaker in order to mix it properly. I tried whisking it with a fork, but it was just disgusting. Find it quite delicious now though, when it's prepared correctly. Jasper and I took our lunch to the pavilion – he had Pedigree biscuits and I had chocolate milkshake in a cool-bottle. Have realised that the pavilion has become my replacement balcony. There's a water fountain there and even a barbeque! Took a book and we laid on the benches and read for an hour. Took my leg for its daily walk around the lake, then home to do the laundry (husband had no clean socks this morning, and sarcastically asked if I could buy him some new ones if I didn't intend doing any laundry!)

FRIDAY 16 MAY

Woke up feeling very 'empty' inside, but I mean physically rather than emotionally, so that's good! Chocolate shakes are very tasty, but only fill you for an hour, so am learning to live with hunger.

Was invited to Rebecca's for drinks this morning. Took a huge box of chocolate doughnuts, but thankfully managed to resist eating one myself. Rebecca tried to insist I took them home again, but of course I refused. Had a lovely time drinking fresh juice and gossiping for an hour, then arrived home to find the husband had finally been successful in obtaining our own internet connection – there was great rejoicing when girls arrived home.

SATURDAY 17 MAY

Another quiet day. Husband needed laptop for work-related matters all morning, and I had yet more laundry – why do I allow it to pile up? The weekdays just fly past and if you lose concentration for only one afternoon, it's domestic chaos. Must try harder. Lulu accused me yesterday of never washing her clothes! Now that I'm feeling better, need to re-focus on domestic routine. Have crystal-clear image in head of self running the house like clockwork, finger on the pulse of everything, with files and folders containing clipped and stapled bills and receipts – a place for everything and everything in its place. But what have I got? Piles and piles of unpacked cardboard boxes, containing goodness only knows what. Think I need a desk. Of my own. From where I can run the household with skill and precision. Think I need a chic leather desk-set, in lime-green mock-crock. And a Mont Blanc pen. And possibly some personal stationery. Feel sure it would help me to focus.

SUNDAY 18 MAY

Whole family was struck by cabin fever at 5.00pm last night, so we went out for dinner to popular Mediterranean restaurant in Narellan. Girls looked stunning, as usual, and everyone in good mood. Began with blue-coloured Fruit Tingle cocktail (me) and garlic bread (everyone else). Girls and I ordered chicken and the husband opted for seafood. Was all delicious, although the naughty husband upset us all by dangling a whole baby octopus on the end of his fork – as Lulu pointed out, you could see its suckers! Still, a large carafe of white wine calmed us down. Upon arriving home, decided to all lie in the parental bed and watch 'Cheaper by the Dozen' for the 10th time. Were all squashed but happy.

WEEK 20
Green Tea and Pink Champagne

MONDAY 19 MAY

Okay, so we all knew I wasn't likely to get the designer leather desk-set, but I've learned how to operate on a limited budget. My lofty aspirations have lowered considerably these last few months. With this in mind, I went to the mall this morning. Found very nice desk set in Lincraft, and have managed to set up desk with minimal expenditure. (Actually, have only borrowed desk from girls, but expect to get my own shortly – as soon as husband can be persuaded to face the crowds in Ikea). Can feel my mind whirring into focus already. I will be the CEO of the Young household. Only problem is, no-one ever obeys my commands, whether it's instructing teenagers to tidy their rooms or asking husband to paint the walls. Must work harder at being more authoritative. Will begin tomorrow.

TUESDAY 20 MAY

I have read somewhere (feel sure it was in a glossy magazine) that Gwyneth Paltrow allegedly loves green tea. And there is an advert running here that shows Nigella promoting green tea while dressed in a very fetching little lime-green cardigan. So, I decided that if it was good enough for Gwyneth and Nigella, I should give it a try.

Had visions of purchasing cute little Maxwell & Williams polka dot teapot, and maybe some tiny little demi-cups and saucers, in order to enhance the experience. Luckily, just stuck to our old Ikea white china mugs, because the tea was SO disgusting! It made me feel sick. I persevered for almost a full mugful, but had to throw it away. Worse still, I could taste it in my throat all night. Was very disappointed. Cannot justify purchasing the cute teapot now. Or the chic little cups. Even more annoying, today I bought the new edition of Instyle magazine and they were running a huge feature on the benefits of drinking tea! I am such a failure. Have to admit though, that it wasn't Twinings, which is what Nigella promotes. Perhaps will have to buy some Twinings and try again. Gwyneth must have very peculiar tastebuds if she really does love green tea.

WEDNESDAY 21 MAY

Well, the jet-setting husband strikes again. There's some big-deal rugby match in Sydney tonight, which apparently ranks in importance along the lines of England v Scotland kind of thing. Think it's Queensland v New South Wales, but couldn't swear to it. Anyway, the husband and his boss are staying in some fancy apartment hotel in Darling Harbour, getting the Rivercat up to the Olympic Stadium, watching the match from some corporate box, Rivercat back and then night on the town in the bars around Darling Harbour. He's promised to telephone and say goodnight – if I have time to speak to him in-between cooking dinner for girls, walking the dog and sweeping the floors. Just call me Cinderella. When will MY jet-set life take off, that's what I want to know.

THURSDAY 22 MAY

Have joined Weight Watchers at Harrington Park. As I was waiting my turn, I half expected to be told I was barred. Honestly, I could probably pay off my mortgage with the amount of joining fees I've paid to slimming clubs. But, I had no choice. I just need the motivation of being monitored every week. Monitoring myself is no good. The chocolate milkshake diet went very well, and I lost the extra pounds gained during those sad few weeks of being housebound. This means I'm back to being one stone lighter than when I arrived here.

Still looked rather a sad case though, as I limped through the door. Can never sleep when the husband is away, so I was very tired this morning. Didn't have time to wash my hair, so scraped it back into a greasy ponytail. Woke up this morning with a sticky eye and realised I had a very bad case of conjunctivitis, and a left eye which looked like a dead fish, so had to wear glasses to meeting instead of contact lenses. Due to poorly leg/back and the need to constantly exercise it, I have to wear trainers every day – not a good look. Also, I was running a little late and grabbed the nearest thing to wear, which turned out to be a dubious hooded top from Kmart which I bought in a jet-lagged panic when our luggage went missing on arrival here. All in all, I was probably the saddest-looking case ever to walk through the Weight Watchers' door, but just think how good the transformation will look. The thought of swimming in the ocean baths has got me back on the straight and narrow. Just have to make sure I stay there.

FRIDAY 23 MAY

I am so naïve. When I reported that the husband was catching the Rivercat ferry up to the rugby match, I completely failed to realise that it was actually a privately chartered CRUISE – where he was fed champagne, wine, beer, oysters, pasta, pancakes, spring rolls, satay sticks etc. etc. etc. I brought him down to earth the next day when I served him a jacket potato for his dinner!

SUNDAY 25 MAY

Have been out jet-setting! At last! Can you believe it? Think the husband was feeling guilty at his excessive gadding about, so he took me to the Food and Wine Festival at Cronulla. There were lots of white marquees selling different wines and champagne and cocktails, and tasty food stalls. There was also a live band playing Roxy Music and soul. We stood on the sea-front watching the surfers while drinking pink champagne and listening to 'Dock of the Bay' at full volume. Now this is the life I had in mind when I agreed to move here – let's hope things are clicking into place at last. (Must just point out though; I was drinking pink champagne, but husband was driving and therefore on diet coke, and Jasper Conran was on water).

WEEK 21
Factory Girl

MONDAY 26 MAY

Husbands can be very slippery creatures. You really have to keep a very close eye on them. It would appear that I have been 'volunteered' to carry out an emergency packing job for an important new customer! The goods will arrive here on Wednesday, and I am to spend the foreseeable future packing 1,000 Gripples, keys and instructions into 1,000 plastic bags. Oh what a glamorous life I do lead.

Obviously someone thought I needed bringing back down to earth after yesterday's jet-setting. Thought just struck me – perhaps yesterday's jet-setting was in order to soften me up for new life as Factory Girl?

TUESDAY 27 MAY

Have spent the last couple of evenings constantly talking to friends and family on new SKYPE connection – a very marvellous invention, but have absolutely no idea how it works, or how it can be so cheap compared to the cost of normal landline calls. Husband tried to explain it to me, but it's completely beyond my comprehension. All I know is that it costs less than 3 cents per minute and, as I explained to the husband, the more time I spend on SKYPE, the more money I'm saving him – it's a very simple equation, but is apparently completely beyond his comprehension.

Must go, need to have a think about what to buy with the money I'm saving on 'phone calls.

WEDNESDAY 28 MAY

The teenagers are in disgrace, yet again. Was expecting delivery of Gripples from Polyplas today, so I placed a notice on front door which read, "DELIVERY DRIVER, PLEASE KNOCK LOUDLY." However, forgot to remove notice after taking possession of package, so when teenagers arrived home, despite neither of them being a delivery driver, or even being in possession of a driving licence, they hammered on the door loudly enough to wake the dead. This sent Jasper Conran charging to the door, barking his head off. I lurched to stop him (being ever mindful of the Indoor Dog Police), tripped over and almost squashed him to death. Pain seared though poorly leg, and I lay in the hallway in a haze of agony and fury. Girls were unable to see what they'd done wrong, but Annie atoned slightly by sticking labels on the Gripple bags for me.

THURSDAY 29 MAY

Have found my vocation, albeit not one of my own choosing. It would appear that I am an excellent Factory Girl. I can coil 50 lengths of 4 metre wire in approximately 45 minutes. Was struggling with new job at first, and was initially very slow and fumbling. Luckily, I remembered my 5th Year economics lessons and applied the 'Division of Labour' principles. Found it much quicker to coil all the wire and label all the bags before beginning to assemble them. Am now speeding through the task at a rate of knots. Have sadly instructed the husband to tell Polyplas to keep my wages in lieu of the recent huge internet bill run up by the girls. There goes my hairdressing money. Damn those teenagers.

119

FRIDAY 30 MAY

Really, I should be in a lager advert, because I PROBABLY have the best working conditions in the world. I stand in the dining room side of the kitchen counter, and I watch The Devil Wears Prada while coiling wire. Jasper Conran sleeps at my feet. I stop for cold drinks and snacks whenever I feel like it, and take a 15 minute break to play Solitaire on the laptop when I feel a bit bored. By 4.45pm I start to panic a bit that the husband will be home shortly and I haven't coiled as many wires as I boldly boasted I would that morning, but I just tell him that I had to stop to wash, iron, cook and clean, and hope that he doesn't check the sock drawer!

SATURDAY 31 MAY

Stayed in all day because Lulu woke up paralysed this morning! It can be bitterly cold in this house some mornings, and I think the chill must have sent her neck muscles into a spasm. The poor little thing lay in bed crying until the husband got up and heard her whimpering. Luckily, the poor child recovered mid-afternoon. Really need to programme central heating to turn on early morning in future. Recent economising is obviously a bit too drastic if it's paralysing the children!

SUNDAY 1 JUNE

Went to Cronulla today. Left girls doing homework, and left Jasper Conran in their care as it was raining and didn't fancy dragging a wet dog around. This meant that husband and I could go into a bar for our lunch and relax for a few hours. Went to bar/restaurant called 'The Point' and shared delicious pizza and fries. Tried not to think about Weight Watchers meeting next Thursday. Realised yesterday, to my dismay, that I was so busy being a Factory Girl last week, I forgot to go to the meeting! I will aim to remember this week. Have given up crisps and chocolate. Again.

WEEK 22
The Devil Wears Kmart

MONDAY 2 JUNE

Woke up this morning absolutely brimming with determination. Need to sort out vast swathes of my life, and also that of husband, girls and dog. From now on, will run our lives with steely determination, and will accept no nonsense from any of them.

Firstly, need to sort out finances. Now that we finally have tenants in our house back home, the UK bills are taken care of for the moment. However, here in Sydney the dollars are constantly zooming out of our bank account. If I go to the Plaza for mushrooms, I come back having spent $23.00! So, to get a grip on this, I have bought an Accounts Book and in this I will write down every single transaction which is made from our bank account. Have drawn up headings for each column, and will analyse exactly where the money goes. Will begin next Monday.

Next, need to plan week's food menu well in advance of supermarket shopping excursion. During my illness, I allowed Darla's excellent influence to slide, and desperately need to regain status as thrifty housewife. Am currently spending approximately $140.00 per week on food, a huge increase from the early months here, and entirely due to my laziness (and illness). Resolved to plan menus every Monday morning in future. Will begin immediately.

Also need to plan diet and exercise routine for the husband. When he was living a bachelor life over here, for 3 months before we joined him, he was SO organised. He used to come home from work each evening, go for a jog round the lake, cook himself a healthy meal such as grilled fish and salad, do his work admin, check his bank account on-line and generally keep his life in good order. These days he come home, does his work admin, eats his meal and collapses on the sofa in front of the tv. This is not good for him. In future, am going to ensure his joggers and trainers are ready for when he arrives home, and will accompany him on swift walk around Harrington Park every evening. (Will also stop buying him any more Cadbury's Fruit and Nut). Will begin immediately.

The teenagers are in dire need of discipline. They've been getting away with murder since we arrived here, mainly because I still feel guilty for ruining their lives (their words, not mine). This cannot continue. Is very bad for them to be so pampered. Have drawn up charts for each girl, showing exactly what chores are expected of them. From now on they will be expected to make their beds without fail, keep bedrooms tidy and organise their own laundry, ready for me to wash. In addition, have decided that they can be responsible for cooking the evening meal once a week. Will begin immediately.

Even Jasper Conran has not escaped my tyrannical regime. Am determined to make him sleep in his basket, instead of in our bed. The husband is getting very cross at waking up to find he's sharing his pillow with a dog (Jasper, not me). Need to start training him to sleep in cage again. Will begin in a couple of weeks, after he's had a chance to get used to the idea. Don't want to upset him by being too harsh too soon.

TUESDAY 3 JUNE

Have realised that if I am to gain respect of the household, then desperately need to smarten up appearance. Cannot expect to be obeyed without question when slobbing around in baggy joggers with no make-up and greasy hair. (Also need to ditch the Kmart clothes!) Need professional help to improve appearance. Decided to go to Plaza and check out the hairdresser next door to supermarket. Managed to get immediate appointment, much to my relief, and was lead to very comfy leather chair which massages body as you're being shampooed! Whole experience was very luxurious and only cost $41.00 for cut and blow-dry. After staring at self in very unforgiving hairdressing mirror for an hour, called in at pharmacy on way home and bought expensive moisturiser. Thank goodness the new Account Book regime is not starting until next week. Need to work harder at controlling impulse spending.

WEDNESDAY 4 JUNE

Was VERY stern with the teenagers tonight, and insisted they could not use the computers until they'd tidied their bedrooms. They tried telling me how they had absolutely GOT to do their homework immediately, but I know this is a euphemism for signing-in to MSN. I summoned up my best Miranda Priestly voice and told them straight, "Tales of your incompetence do not interest me." When I checked bedrooms later, I discovered that Annie had simply scooped everything off the floor and thrown it into the laundry basket, and Lulu had scooped everything off the floor, thrown it on her bed and covered it up with the duvet. Need to work harder at controlling naughty teenagers.

THURSDAY 5 JUNE

Went to Weight Watchers this morning. They are all so friendly and not at all patronising. They didn't even charge me for missing last week. Australian people are so kind. Anyway, was delighted to be told I'd lost 2lbs. Not much I know, but better than nothing. Took Jasper round the lake with a spring in my step today, and planned exercise routine for the husband. Came home and packed yet more Gripples. Only another 200 to go now.

FRIDAY 6 JUNE

Decided to get dressed-up today as if going out for lunch – instead of simply packing Gripples all day. Did hair and make-up, put on chic linen trousers and cashmere jumper, painted nails etc. Was very pleased with whole effect, and felt very elegant and ladylike. Took dog outside for toilet and, after spinning around 3 times, he was sick on my foot! Had to shower feet and sandals. Need to take more careful note of direction in which dog is facing next time he's been eating grass. He obviously has rather strong projectile vomiting muscles for such a small dog.

SATURDAY 7 JUNE

Quite a boring day, really. Husband decided to sort out his study and spent all morning and half the afternoon tidying and filing. I did some laundry and tidied out my wardrobe. Bit depressed to be reminded that I have lots and lots of clothes that are still too small for me. Need to step up diet and exercise into another gear. Will soon be spring and then summer, and simply must be thin by then. Will begin on Monday.

SUNDAY 8 JUNE

Yet another quiet day. Girls were busy with homework assignments all day, so the planned family day out was cancelled. Spent a couple of hours surfing the internet, looking-up Net-a-Porter, Hobbs and L K Bennett. Need inspiration to stiffen resolve to work harder at diet and exercise. Went out for a ride in the truck with husband late afternoon, and finally saw a wild kangaroo! Two of them in fact. They were eating grass by the side of the road. Cannot think why I've been so worried by them. They were really cute little things and barely reached the height of the wheels. Suspect the fully-fledged adults are a different matter though.

WEEK 23
Dental and Dietary Disasters

MONDAY 9 JUNE

Bank Holiday today, in honour of the Queen's birthday. Girls could not be bothered to get ready to go out, so husband and I went off by ourselves. Drove to Berrima, a small Georgian town in the Southern Highlands which was established in 1831. When we first pulled up in the car park, I almost thought we were back in England – these rural villages look like either a Wild West town or a Yorkshire Dales village! The gaol in Berrima was established by 1840 and since that time has held criminals, mariners, internees and German prisoners of war, and today it's a Women's Correctional Centre. Must be a very spooky place to sleep in. Just the thought of staying there would be enough to keep me on the straight and narrow.

Went in all the gift shops, but my favourite was a little bookbinding shop which sold lovely stationery. Was angling for a very sophisticated black and white pen for my desk (vital to the efficient running of the household) but husband was pretending to be deaf. If the Accounts Book is not up-to-date this week for lack of a suitable pen, on his head be it.

Enjoyed drinks and cakes in cosy little patisserie before driving home through the Royal National Park – husband did NOT forewarn me before turning off main highway and heading into the forest. Was quite cross, but route was not too alarming. On way home, husband announced he thinks he'd have made a good explorer back in the 1800's, and he'd have liked to go to sea. He was terribly hurt by my scoffing that it was a very bold statement to make from the comfort of his luxury 4x4! He'd have been keel-hauled within an hour of leaving port.

TUESDAY 10 JUNE

Lulu's birthday today. It was a very different day to her previous UK birthdays – the limousine was notable by its absence! We gave her books, chocolates and money for a digital camera. She also received a wad of money by post from Grandma, and a watercolour set from her cousins. I'd ordered a chocolate mud cake from the patisserie, and when I collected it the kind lady gave the 'one' and 'four' candles free. We ordered pizzas from Pizza Hut for supper and everybody chose a special stuffed crust instead of the usual bargain deal. (Strictly speaking, they all have bargain deals, Jasper and I always have a stuffed crust). After pizza, Caesar salad and chocolate cake, we watched tv. Worst part of the day for Lulu was having only three non-singers serenade her with happy birthday – being such a small crowd, none of us could get away with only mouthing the words!

WEDNESDAY 11 JUNE

Final consignment of Gripple bags arrived this afternoon, so now I have no excuse for not cracking-on with the packing. Was reluctant to begin again as cannot wind wire fast enough while wearing the special rubber 'Ninja' gloves provided, and without them I keep getting tiny shards of metal stuck in my fingers.

New, stringent, household accounting procedure was shot to pieces today. Have had double dental disaster. Girls had routine check-up appointments, which were $45.00 each and accounted for. However, it was discovered that Annie has a small 'pitt' in the back of her front tooth which needs a specialist filler, and Lulu needed an x-ray to find out what's happening with an adult tooth in her top jaw. So, the final bill at reception was $200.00. It will also cost

$60.00 on Saturday for Annie's filling. Am devastated. Not much chance of getting my highlights done now.

THURSDAY 12 JUNE

Packing, packing, packing. Factory life is boring me somewhat now. Watched '27 Dresses' and 'Failure to Launch' while packing today. Was very cross to realise that I forgot to go to Weight Watchers again. Cannot keep doing this. Is ridiculous to only go every fortnight, and disastrous for my willpower.

FRIDAY 13 JUNE

Yet more dental disasters. The husband had appointment for consultation about a cracked tooth (it was cracked before we left the UK and temporarily patched-up, but was warned that this would only last a few months). New dentist has re-patched the crack again (over $100.00) and informed him that he needs a crown as soon as possible ($1,100.00). However, he was watching tv tonight when a large filling fell out from another tooth. Goodness only knows what that will cost to replace.

SATURDAY 14 JUNE

Annie and her father went cheerily off to the dentist together, and returned home having spent only $60.00, thank goodness. Kind dentist did not charge the husband for temporary filling, but it will be a large bill when he has it done properly in three weeks' time. Damn teeth.

Husband, Lulu and I were just about to get in truck to go and buy digital camera, when Lulu's friend texted to ask if she wanted to go shopping. Lulu was in a quandary, so I suggested we dropped her at the mall to meet friend, and husband and I went to buy camera. Lulu leapt at suggestion, so off we went.

Had to queue for almost an hour at camera shop. Was very disconcerted when one of the assistants produced a camera with a

HUGE lens and took a photo of the queue – and I was right at the front of it! If I appear on some billboard in the city, I will sue.

Thankfully, after waiting all that time we managed to buy the cool lime-green camera she wanted. Also had to buy a memory card, so total bill was $300.00. It has been a very expensive week.

Felt in need of a little sustenance, so bought a bottle of raspberry Sparkletini on way home. There's nothing like spending money to cheer you up when you're feeling down after spending too much money!

SUNDAY 15 JUNE

Very boring day. Packed Gripples all day until 3.00pm when husband and I went for our usual circular drive. We drive through Cobbitty, along the wildlife corridor and out into the countryside until we come to Picton, then home through Razorback and into Camden. Made spaghetti Bolognese for dinner, then spent a few hours on Skype. Late to bed and guiltily realised had forgotten to iron husband's work shirt. Must try harder to be more organised. Will begin tomorrow.

WEEK 24
Elephant Lady

MONDAY 16 JUNE

The more organised week got off to a very bad start – yet again. Saw family off to work and school, laid down on bed with JC to plan power-walking route, and woke up with a start at 12.35pm!!! Must not let this happen tomorrow. Rushed down to Plaza to pay the rent money, and suddenly thought, "Why am I rushing? What do I have to hurry for? I really should CALM DOWN." So, I bought In-Style magazine and had lunch at Michel's Patisserie. Felt very calm and centred afterwards, so strolled home and took Jasper Conran for a leisurely walk around the lake before preparing dinner for family.

Lulu went on a field trip to Chinatown today. She saw lots of buildings and monuments of historical and geographical significance, but was most impressed by the Hello Kitty shop, and is working out when she can get there again for a shopping spree!

TUESDAY 17 JUNE

Had a little expedition today. Desperately needed new cable for computer monitor, so walked into Narellan town centre. Was a bit of a scary walk, with lorries thundering past me. Was also a bit swampy underfoot in places, and had to walk alongside a ditch for quite a long stretch. Kept a wary eye out for snakes and spiders. Jeans are quite flared, and I was worried something might run up my leg! Wanted to turn back, but eventually made it safely into town – threat of being without means of cheap communication was enough to keep me going! Bought new monitor cable (and Vogue) and was back home within the hour. Might do this regularly now that I know the way – the newsagent in Narellan has an excellent selection of magazines that are well worth risking life and limb for!

WEDNESDAY 18 JUNE

Woke up at 5.00am to find right hand in searing agony. Went to bathroom and found hand covered in bites, some of which were bleeding copiously. Didn't dare go back to sleep in case fell into coma and died, so waited half an hour then woke up husband. He was very concerned and said I must go to doctors as soon as surgery opened. This worried me even more, because the husband usually dismisses my ailments.

Anyway, went to surgery at 8.00am and only had to wait 10 minutes. Very kind Chinese doctor doesn't "think" it's fatal, because he would expect to see more 'sweating' around a fatal wound. Let's hope he's right.

Had a long nap this afternoon. Hand still numb and bites grew ever more horrific-looking as the day wore on. They're now all bleeding and oozing clear gungy liquid.

Some good news though, is that newspaper announced today that Australian scientists believe they have found a cure for bird flu. I was SO relieved, I almost cried. In the event of a pandemic being announced, a mass vaccination will take place – starting with the Prime Minister. At last there's now a vacancy on my Worry List.

THURSDAY 19 JUNE

Another disastrous day. Woke up to find I was the proud owner of a hand which wouldn't look out of place attached to the arm of John Merrick! At least it's stopped bleeding though, so must be getting better. Looks like the Chinese doctor was right about it not being fatal, thank goodness.

Went to wake girls up for school and discovered Lulu was struck by another case of paralysed neck syndrome, and was weeping with pain. She had an important English exam this afternoon, so we agreed that she'd rest for a couple of hours and then get moving. Luckily this worked, and Rebecca kindly gave her a lift to school at 12.30pm. Why is their father never at home when there is a crisis???

All this drama meant that I missed Weight Watchers YET AGAIN. Would have been willing to attend with grotesque hand on show, but couldn't leave sick child. Why are my efforts always sabotaged? Now I have the dilemma that it will be cheaper to rejoin than pay back-fees for the missed classes. Cannot afford all this wasted expense. Am deeply depressed.

FRIDAY 20 JUNE

Am now in constant state of terror. MRI scan is on Monday at 10.15am. Cannot sleep for worrying, and when I do manage to sleep I wake in panic from hideous claustrophobic nightmares. Have buried head in sand for last two months, but cannot ignore the issue any longer. I want to back out and just not turn-up. However, if I don't go now, I will have to pay for the scan (over $500.00) as they require notice of cancellation, and Medicare won't pay out good money for me being a wimp. Also, husband says that if I don't go, he will never again take me out for a Sunday drive. Feel like my whole life is on hold until the scan is over and done with.

SATURDAY 21 JUNE

Have looked up MRI scans on Google Images. Now in worse state than before. Damn the internet and its wealth of easily accessible information.

SUNDAY 22 JUNE

Lovely husband took me for day out to Cronulla to take mind off MRI scan troubles. Did not work. Still terrified.

WEEK 25
Reprieve at the 11th Hour

MONDAY 23 JUNE

Someone IS on my side after all. Had sleepless night due to worry over scan – heart racing, hands trembling, legs shaking, crying etc. etc. etc. We were due to leave the house at 9.45am, and at 9.35am was just drying hair when clinic rang to say the appointment was cancelled. Apparently, their equipment had failed due to a power surge.

Was initially overjoyed at cancellation of scan, but am now really cross as it would have all been over with by now. New appointment is for 21 July, and that's a long time to wait in a state of anxiety yet again.

TUESDAY 24 JUNE

Jasper Conran is out of control. Made him sleep in cage last night, as cannot cope any longer with three of us permanently in the marital bed. Well, he had me up four times, scrabbling at his cage to wake me. I always think he might need the toilet, so I open the cage door carefully and attach his lead to take him outside, but he just tries to bolt through the bathroom and into my bedroom. After getting up for the fourth time, I let him into bed. Have been absolutely exhausted today. Feels like having a newborn baby again. Husband suggested putting his cage in the garage, but I can't do that to him as far too cold in there. Really don't want dog having paralysed neck, in addition to teenager. Will see how it goes tonight.

WEDNESDAY 25 JUNE

Has been a very bad day today. Lulu was sent home with severe migraine. The husband was nearby so he collected her, and she was sick all over the rear seats. Impending pain might explain her foul temper this morning; she got in the truck and threw her sandwich into the back seat – it bounced off her father's head and landed in the footwell. She also threw her planner, which narrowly missed her sister who was cowering in the corner. It was very hard to be angry with her this afternoon when she was in such agony. She's hoping to be better for the athletics carnival at school tomorrow.

Better night with Jasper Conran last night. He only woke me up once, and I banged on the top of his cage with my hand, which sent him scuttling back to his bed and he never moved again until the alarm went off at 6.30am. Let's hope he's getting the message.

Husband not in a good mood tonight – brought on by me asking him to take me on FOUR errands! Went to Plaza to buy fresh salad, then again for fresh bread, then to library in Narellan and finally back to Plaza again for refreshments for girls to take to athletics carnival tomorrow. He's just a little bit cross with me, so I'm keeping a very low profile tonight!

THURSDAY 26 JUNE

Feel sure my leg is practically cured. It doesn't hurt at all (well, except when sitting down for any length of time) and I feel so much better. Took Jasper Conran round the lake this morning (he was besieged by a gang of toddlers shouting, "Puppy, puppy,") then took him home and went for long power walk, right round the perimeter of the Lakeside Village.

FRIDAY 27 JUNE

Jasper Conran tricked me last night, and husband was very, very cross with me. JC was scrabbling in his cage, and it was getting towards morning so I thought that perhaps he needed the toilet. I let him out of the cage and before I could put his lead on, he dived under the bed! There was nothing I could do, so I just got back into bed, but when the alarm went off at 6.30am, he was snuggled down in the middle of the bed with his head on the husband's pillow! I don't see how I can possibly be held responsible for what happens when I am half asleep, but the husband was cross with me all day.

Had a bit of a lie-in this morning. Didn't go back to sleep, just had a long think and a bit of a worry about life. Spent the afternoon sorting out shopping lists and menus for the week. Also drafted diet plan (which revolves around three low-fat meals per day) and power walking schedule.

This evening Lulu has kindly highlighted my roots for me. Turned out fine (from a distance, with no contact lenses) and saved me a fortune.

SATURDAY 28 JUNE

Am very cross, yet again, with the teenagers. I wanted to have a family outing to Featherdale Wildlife Park, where you can get up-close with the kangaroos and koalas. Naughty girls though, just wanted to laze around the house watching tv and could not be bothered to get ready. We eventually left them in charge of the dog, with enough money to buy a Pot Noodle, and went out by ourselves.

We drove through the countryside to Picton, and had a late lunch at a restaurant which is situated in a converted Post Office. We sat on a small private balcony for two, and I had chicken salad while the husband had grilled chicken on toasted Turkish bread. The greedy little piggy also had a Devonshire cream tea afterwards, which consisted of two huge scones and pots of jam and cream.

Renewed dieting determination prevented me from indulging in toffee cheesecake.

SUNDAY 29 JUNE

Finally managed to persuade the girls to participate in family day out. They got ready while husband and I prepared picnic. Calm prevailed until we got in the truck, when all hell suddenly broke loose! To begin with, Annie refused to sit in the spot where Lulu had been sick earlier in the week, but her sister refused to swap with her as she didn't want to sit in the sick spot either. Eventually calmed them down and we set off, only for hell to break loose yet again – this time over a bag of Gummi Bears! Had bought two bags but mistakenly only put one in the car, and of course at age 14 and 15 they couldn't possibly be expected to share their sweets without arguing. Felt like we'd been in the truck for hours before we'd even left the estate.

Decided to go to Bulli Point and check-out the viewing platform, from which we've heard you can see for miles. Well, it was VERY scary. The platform juts way out over the cliff and as soon as you step onto it, your stomach plunges. Jasper Conran was not happy and shot backwards to escape. Views were indeed spectacular, and you could see right down the coastline beyond Wollongong.

We ate our picnic and then walked along the little forest paths. Family thought it was very funny to scream, "SNAKE," and watch my reaction. (Apparently, I jumped around on tippy-toes, all thoughts of damaged spinal discs abandoned).

Drove down the coast to Wollongong, but girls couldn't be bothered to get out of the car, so we didn't stay long. Called at McDonalds to stock up on frozen coke and McFlurries for the drive home.

WEEK 26
The Invisible Mother

MONDAY 30 JUNE

First day of the school holidays, and already the teenagers are bored. However, I have got a programme of revision lined-up, but will wait a few days before revealing it. The next three weeks are going to be such fun!

TUESDAY 1 JULY

Lulu was invited to Grand Union Cinema at Campbelltown with a group of friends, but had no lift, so we had to check out the buses for the first time. Downloaded timetable and maps from the internet, and we set off at 10.15am this morning. Was a piece of cake. We were at Macarthur Square within 30 minutes. Problem was, Lulu went to meet chums, and I had SIX HOURS to kill – by myself.

I was under very strict instructions that if I happened to bump into her and her friends, UNDER NO CIRCUMSTANCES was I to acknowledge her or give any indication whatsoever that I might be her mother! So, as she was coming up the escalator as I was going down, I looked the other way. When I was sitting by the fountain enjoying a drink and reading a magazine, I pretended not to see them stroll past me. Finally, when she was sitting on the steps with two girls at 5.00pm waiting for a lift home from her father, I waited behind a pillar, firmly out of sight until he arrived – and then got told off because the other girls were only waiting with her so she wouldn't be alone until I arrived!

Teenagers – you just can't win.

WEDNESDAY 2 JULY

Very quiet day. Stuck to diet all day. Long power walk with JC.

THURSDAY 3 JULY

Once again, the teenagers are out of control. Husband got up for work at 6.30am this morning, to find the naughty girls just going to bed!!! They'd been on MSN all night to friends in UK. This happens every single school holiday. Within 4 days they've become nocturnal and are back on UK time.

At least Jasper and I had a very peaceful day without them – until they finally surfaced at 4.00pm. In future, I am taking the internet connections to bed with me.

FRIDAY 4 JULY

Am suffering with the worst cold in the history of the common cold. Couldn't sleep last night, as couldn't breathe when lying down, so feel very wretched today. Husband has just been to Aldi to buy the weekend groceries and called at the Bottle Shop to buy me a bottle of wine. Am going to sit down with a nice cold glass of wine and a plate of homemade lasagne – yummy!

SATURDAY 5 JULY

Still poorly.

SUNDAY 6 JULY

Still poorly but decided to allow husband to take me for a drive, as very bored stuck in house. Left the teenagers in bed (at 1.30pm!)

and set off. Was very funny when we first got in the truck, as Jasper Conran refused to sit in the sicky seat – every time we put him on the seat, he threw himself on the floor and almost throttled himself with his seat belt. Had to give in and put him at the other side, behind me.

Went to Whale Beach, as the whales have been in the harbour and around the Northern Beaches recently, but they weren't out today. Carried on up to Palm Beach and took a couple of photos. Had a nice afternoon but the husband was fed-up with me because I've got a temperature and insisted on having the air-conditioning on full-blast, so he was shivering throughout the whole journey.

WEEK 27
Crash Landing at Cape Canaveral

MONDAY 7 JULY

Still very sick with bad cold. Stayed indoors all day. Teenagers spent all day at Cape Canaveral – husband's new name for the study, brought about by the excessive amount of communications equipment in there. At the last count there was one desk-top pc, three laptops, three headsets, two webcams, three cameras and two ipods. They spend all day on MSN with Australian kids, and all night on MSN with British kids, and sleep from approximately 6.00am – 1.00pm, then begin again. I suspect they're taking advantage of my latest illness. Must get a grip tomorrow.

TUESDAY 8 JULY

Am too sick to write. Cannot breathe through stuffy nose. Have used a whole box of tissues. Teenagers manned Mission Control all day and night, yet again. Am definitely going to get a grip tomorrow. They need to begin their school assignments.

WEDNESDAY 9 JULY

Disastrous day. Was furious with the teenagers when I discovered them on MSN – messaging each other from across the room! Was just about to make them shut down the computers and do something productive when the main laptop crashed and died, quickly followed by Lulu's laptop. Looks like there is a major bug in the system. My desktop is still out of action due to faulty monitor, so we are now down to one, very slow, laptop. We've lost all our email addresses and photos and have no Skype connection. I feel abandoned in the wilderness.

THURSDAY 10 JULY

Lulu's laptop has been partially resuscitated (working, but no internet), but the main laptop is definitely dead.

FRIDAY 11 JULY

Life without computers is surprisingly good. We all sit down to watch tv together, and we talk more. Today, Annie has been to the mall with her friends, and Lulu has been painting. I've been shopping to Camden and bought a bedside table for Lulu (only $10.00).

While browsing in the second-hand bookshop I picked up a book about sorting out your money, and was a little discomfited when I read the first paragraph. It detailed how we all waste money on things we can do without, and used MAGAZINES as an example! It said that you buy a magazine and when you've read it, it's useless and is then thrown away. You would NEVER take a $5.00 note out of your purse and throw it in the bin, but that's effectively what you're doing!!!

Have made a hard decision. HAVE RENOUNCED MAGAZINES FOR EVER. (Thank goodness I'm stocked up with all the current editions). Should also point out that the author is far behind the times – no way can you buy a magazine for $5.00 these days. Don't tell the husband, but I paid $15.00 for American Vogue last week!

SATURDAY 12 JULY

We are decorating! Well, strictly speaking, the husband is decorating, but I'm being very helpful by pointing out the gaps every time he misses a bit (I just ignore the swearing). We're decorating Annie's bedroom to begin with, and are just painting it all completely white. I've bought some black faux-fur to make a new throw for the bed, which should look very nice with the red and white cushions. Husband has mended the wonky shelves and put new handles on the wardrobe. Hopefully, by this time tomorrow it should all be finished.

While I was at the bookshop yesterday, I bought "I Don't Know How She Does It" by Allison Pearson. There is nothing decent left in the library, so I've resorted to re-reading books I enjoyed years ago. Hope it's as good as I remember.

SUNDAY 13 JULY

Everyone up very early this morning to finish the painting. (Stictly speaking, husband finished the actual painting while I read, "I Don't Know How She Does It.") The room looks lovely and Annie is very pleased with it. She's been warned that it had better stay neat and tidy and not degenerate into a disaster zone again.

Went out for our customary Sunday drive once the husband had finished washing all the decorating equipment, and found a beautiful housing estate called Nangarin Vineyard Estate. Drove round it in awe of all the beautiful houses, and dreamed how nice it would be to live there. However, googled it when I returned home and discovered there was a deadly bushfire there a few years ago, and a number of houses were lost. It's easy to forget how deadly Australia can be, when you get carried away by the spectacular setting.

WEEK 28
I Don't Know How She Does Nothing

MONDAY 14 JULY

Am feeling a bit depressed, and it's all the fault of that damned book. I'd forgotten what a stir it caused the first time around. Kate Reddy fits more into a day than I fit into a whole month. It's times like this that make me question my existence. What is the point of me??? Why did I decide to be a stay-at-home mother??? Why don't I have a career??? I used to be very ambitious. I used to have a career. But now I'm on the scrapheap. I always say that I stayed at home with the children because I couldn't bear to leave them, but truthfully I'm pretty sure it was because I knew I'd never manage to get two babies fed and dressed and out the door on time, as well as managing to do my hair and make-up. It was one or the other, and I couldn't possibly go to work looking a mess! So, while Kate Reddy goes to work at a merchant bank, I stay home and do nothing.

TUESDAY 15 JULY

Have decided that I really MUST start fitting more into my day. It appears that the more time you have on your hands, the less you achieve, so I need to keep on the go ALL THE TIME in order to achieve more.

So, today I washed three loads of laundry, cleared a basket of ironing, cleaned the bathrooms, swept all the floors, walked the dog, did a power-walk and paid the rent. Realised that I've been neglecting my patchwork since I lost my balcony so tonight, instead of sitting idly in front of the tv, I completed a huge section of patching. Must keep this up tomorrow. Have instructed the husband to wake me up when he goes to work. Must get up and be productive instead of snoozing until noon.

<u>WEDNESDAY 16 JULY</u>

Keeping busy is really quite exhausting. Got up at 9.00am. (Obviously not the 7.30am I was aiming for, but a huge improvement upon noon). Tidied, washed and ironed, walked dog, power-walked self then, to my intense relief, a parcel arrived for Lulu – her dvds from Amazon. Lulu INSISTED that I sit down with her to watch them. We began with "In Her Shoes" and then moved onto "The Holiday." Was a peaceful afternoon and was just congratulating self on having a day without spending any money when we heard a bell ringing – THE ICE-CREAM MAN! Lulu grabbed the dog while I sprinted out of the door and down the street. Ice-cream man was very friendly and chatty and told me all about the problems with his van, and how it keeps breaking down. When I finally turned to look at the selection board, I realised that he wasn't your everyday ice-cream cornet kind of man, but only sold in BULK. You could buy a pack of 10 Magnums or 20 Cornettos etc, but two little cones were out of the question. We don't have the freezer capacity to cope with this quantity, and I didn't want to disappoint the nice man, so in desperation I bought the smallest item on the menu – a $6.50 tub of honey and macadamia nut ice-cream. We had to eat it all at once due to freezer restrictions – very delicious. Tried to feel guilty about sitting around watching films and eating ice-cream, but failed miserably. (Suspect Kate Reddy would have given her right arm to be in my shoes today). Will resume the non-stop activity tomorrow.

THURSDAY 17 JULY

Got up at 9.00am (am so proud of self). Suspect naughty teenagers had not been in bed very long, as they were both dead to the world. Tidied house, then took Mr Conran for a long walk. Don't think poor old Jasper likes the new 'busy' me very much, because he just follows me around hoping I'll sit down so he can sit on my knee. He eventually gave up and went off to lick the husband's pillow for an hour.

Anyway, in the spirit of my new regime of Keeping On The Go All The Time, I decided to go shopping, and caught the bus to Macarthur Square. The only problem is that this wasn't really in-keeping with the spirit of my other new regime of Not Spending Any Money. But, I figured, what the hell, keeping to one resolution out of two is pretty good going, and I had a great time. Bought Annie a new duvet cover and Lulu a set of drawers on wheels so she can tidy up some of the debris in her bedroom. Had a very leisurely lunch under a white parasol in the square (smoked salmon salad) and bought a paper to read instead of a magazine – thereby saving around $8.00. Husband collected me from the mall at 6.00pm, and reached home to find the teenagers had not long emerged from their beds. Must keep a closer eye on them tonight.

FRIDAY 18 JULY

A minor miracle has occurred. Took Lulu shopping for school shoes this afternoon and managed to find a pair of which we both approved within less than 15 minutes. The whole operation was over with and we were on our way home again in less than half-an-hour. This has never happened before in 12 years of school shoe shopping. (Didn't dare tell the husband that it actually had a lot to do with letting her choose a very expensive pair of designer shoes that cost three times what we paid for the previous ones!)

SATURDAY 19 JULY

Had a very scary day. Have only just calmed down. It all started this morning when Annie asked me to highlight her hair. She had it cut yesterday for the first time in six months, and was desperate for the highlights refreshing. After the success of the previous home-highlighting session on my own hair, Lulu and I mistakenly thought that we were actually trained hairdressers.

Dashed down to Plaza to buy a kit, and merrily set about adding in blonde highlights. Left her the requisite 20 minutes, then almost fainted when she came back from washing out the dye. You could see the bright yellow/gold splodges from 20 paces. My heart was POUNDING. She was almost in tears and was going to cancel her afternoon out with friends. However, once she'd dried it properly the colour seemed to calm down and blend in a bit more. In the end, she curled her hair with the GHDs and this disguised the splodges even more. By the time she went out of the door, you wouldn't even notice anything different about it, and it only cost $15.00 as opposed to $80.00 at the Plaza, so it was well worth the temporary anquish. (Wonder what I could buy with the $65.00 I saved?)

SUNDAY 20 JULY

Culture-filled day today. Been to Botany Bay and stood in the EXACT spot where Captain Cook landed in 1770. Botany Bay is now very industrialised, although still quite picturesque if you look to the left and not to the right - a desalination plant is being built there (amidst great opposition) and is quite an eyesore. You can still see across to the city though, and it also appears to be in a direct flight path to the runway at Kingsford Smith Airport. It was quite scary, actually. You can hear the aeroplanes before you see them, and they're so close you feel you can practically touch them! It was very disconcerting to see how many arrive in a very short space of time – it almost looked like a 'plane would be landing before the previous one was off the runway!

WEEK 29
Jasper Conran is a Fat Dog

MONDAY 21 JULY

The scan is finally over – and I have survived. I suppose my survival was never really in any doubt, but it certainly felt like it to me. Couldn't sleep last night for worrying. Was still awake at 3.10am, and had just dropped off when Lulu woke me at 6.20am requesting that I straighten her hair for her. Bless the little darling.

Arrived at the clinic at 10.00am. Could barely walk into reception as my legs were shaking so much. I was in tears in the waiting room and I think the other patients probably thought I'd been given bad news, as they all cast very sympathetic glances at me. Didn't enlighten them that I was, in fact, just a pathetic wimp.

The nurse called me through at about 10.20am, and she made the husband stay in reception – I was devastated. She showed me into a cubicle and I had to undress and put on a paper gown. Nurse attempted to take my blood pressure, but my arm was shaking so much she had difficulty getting the cuff on it! The anaesthetist came through and the nurse whispered to him, so he knelt down and spoke very kindly to me – in the manner of speaking to a five year old child! I cheered up considerably when he said that my head would not need to go in the machine, and I walked into the x-ray room quite jauntily – until the radiographer confirmed that my head would DEFINITELY be inside the machine.

They laid me out on the stretcher attached to the scanner, and put a canula into my arm. I never flinched at that and the anaesthetist remarked that I was very brave. I boldly informed him that I was used to having needles in my arm, and he looked at me very sternly and obviously thought I was confessing to being a junkie! Had to explain that I mean I've had hundreds of thyroid function tests over the last 12 years!

Anyway, they started to inject the sedative into me, and put an oxygen mask over my face. I whipped the mask straight off and sat up, explaining patiently that I didn't think I could go through with it and I was going to get dressed. They laid me back down and obviously shot the sedative in very quickly because I immediately felt very woozy. They gave me a panic button to hold, (which was really quite foolish of them), and sent me off into the scanner.

I lasted about 30 seconds before I pressed the panic button, and they came running in and pulled me out. Obviously they had severely underestimated the extent of my claustrophobia, and therefore the exact amount of sedative to use on me. From the look on the anaesthetist's face though, he wasn't going to make the same mistake twice. And luckily for me he didn't, because I don't remember anything from that moment until I woke up in the recovery bay. They led me back to the cubicle to get dressed, and then handed me back to the husband in reception. I'm sure the nurse was laughing as she walked away!

I don't remember walking back to the truck, or the journey home, or getting into bed with Mr Conran. I woke up at 3.00pm, just before the girls arrived home from school. Lulu had called at the Plaza and bought me a packet of cheese twisties and a bottle of Diet Coke – bless the little darling.

TUESDAY 22 JULY

I am SO furious. My anger knows no bounds. Took JC to the lake this morning, and a little girl came running up to stroke him, hotly pursued by her mother who snatched up the child and told her in a very loud voice that she must "NEVER touch a pregnant dog because it might bite!" I gave her one of my special looks and walked away. Jasper seemed a bit down all afternoon.

WEDNESDAY 23 JULY

Still very cross. Jasper is NOT a fat dog. These people don't seem to realise that he is just very stocky, with a manly, muscly chest and slightly short legs. Took him for an extra walk today though – a bit more exercise won't harm him. Also realised with horror that his booster injections are long overdue – should have been done in April. Rang the vet and made appointment for Friday.

FRIDAY 25 JULY

Been to vet. Jasper Conran is officially a fat dog. He is now on the Slim Fit programme and has a target weight of 8kg. He currently weighs 9.47kg. Haven't told him his target weight, so as not to depress him with the enormity of the amount he has to lose. He needs to take it one gram at a time. Paid $50.00 for special diet food. He is only allowed 85g of kibble daily, to be split between two meals. He finished tonight's allowance within ten seconds and cried all night outside the laundry room door, which is where we keep his food. He's returning to be weighed by vet again in two weeks.

Received my scan results today. They were in an envelope marked, "To be opened only by referring consultant," but opened them anyway. From what I can gather, the report didn't look too bad. The bottom three discs are not brilliant, and one or two of them have bulges, but didn't sound too drastic. Also have something called "Degenerative Facet Joint Disease," and discovered (during Googling session) that this means the fluid in the joints is drying-up and is a result of "ageing!" Fear am now turning into a dried-up old stick. Very depressed.

SATURDAY 26 JULY

Had a brilliant day. The lovely husband is worried about me, and wanted to cheer me up, so took us to Double Bay. Bought Lulu a very fashionable waistcoat and Annie a cardigan and t-shirt. Went to the fabulous stationery shop and bought birthday present for Lulu's friend. Bought nothing for self, as usual, but we did call at the Chocolate Café and enjoyed white chocolate cheesecake covered with melted chocolate. Love my lovely husband.

SUNDAY 27 JULY

The husband is in BIG trouble with me. Our next door neighbour moved out recently. She's been a widow for many years and has apparently been seeing a man for some time and decided to move in with him. This means she's now renting her house out. Today, three student nurses have moved into Julie's house – all very pretty, petite and Chinese. Consequently, the husband has spent all afternoon wondering if they'll think he looks like a "handy sort of DIY chap," and whether they'll ask him round to help with any 'emergency odd jobs.' Am not very amused with him. However, am secretly not too worried, because if they have to wait as long as I do for him to fix my 'emergency odd jobs,' they will have long graduated by the time he gets round to sorting it!

Lulu has been to a birthday party today, at a large house in the countryside near Picton. It was situated on numerous acres of land, and had horses and a swimming pool in the back garden. Apparently, all her friends are very rich, and she says there is no way she's inviting any of them back to our "little shed!" At least she had a good time, bless her.

WEEK 30
Ankle Weights and Audrey Hepburn

MONDAY 28 JULY

Had a major panic this morning. When we were out driving around the countryside yesterday, we saw lots of calves and lambs, and I thought how sweet they were. Suddenly realised though, that this means it's now Spring and therefore Summer is just around the corner!

I AM NOT READY FOR SUMMER! Have not resolved the sunhat situation nor the swimsuit crisis. Why have I wasted the winter months?

TUESDAY 29 JULY

Have taken drastic action. Bought a 'walking kit' which was on sale in the Plaza (only $8.00). It consists of a belt bag, water bottle, pedometer and ankle weights. Wonder if I could make some little weighted saddle-bags for Jasper Conran, in order to maximise his exercise as well as mine?

WEDNEDAY 30 JULY

Walked for miles today, right round the Hillside Village and twice round the lake. Jasper exhausted. My legs are sore where the ankle weights have rubbed my delicate skin. Must wear long socks tomorrow.

THURSDAY 31 JULY

Don't possess any long socks, so had to borrow the husbands. Did not look very elegant, but needs must.

FRIDAY 1 AUGUST

Am very excited. Woolworths are stocking Diet Coke with Lime – my favourite drink. Bought four bottles, but could not find a fresh lime to go with them. Can get coconuts, ugly fruit, mangoes, practically anything you can think of – but no fresh limes.

Strained atmosphere at home this evening. Annie was grounded for not keeping her bedroom tidy and not putting enough commitment into her studies. Instead of being out at the cinema with her friends, she was in her bedroom with Shakespeare!

SATURDAY 2 AUGUST

Dropped girls at Macarthur Square. Annie is still grounded but Lulu needed someone to go shopping with, as she slept-in and missed her friends, so I reluctantly allowed her to go out. Husband and I went into the city to buy posters for Lulu's bedroom, and came away with two huge Audrey Hepburn posters. She goes on a school trip to Melbourne on Tuesday, and we're going to decorate her room while she's away. (Strictly speaking, husband will be doing the actual decorating, but Jasper and I will be encouraging).

SUNDAY 3 AUGUST

Busy day sorting out Lulu's clothes for Melbourne. Husband gardening. Went for ride out late afternoon and finally saw loads of wild kangaroos. They were hopping across the fields to join their chums who were standing under the trees.

WEEK 31
Jasper Conran is Slimmer of the Week

MONDAY 4 AUGUST

JC and I had a bit of a lie-in this morning. My trapped nerve appears to have flared-up again, and I swallowed tonnes of anti-inflammatories and painkillers last night, so perhaps that's why I was drowsy. Don't know what Jasper's excuse was!

Lulu had major trauma tonight over choice of suitcase for trip tomorrow. Actually, the trauma was due to the fact that she does not possess a Ripcurl/Roxy-type suitcase to take to Melbourne, and had to make do with the budget case we brought from home. She's packed enough clothes to last a fortnight, never mind four days.

Set alarm for 5.00am tomorrow to get ready to wave Lulu off. Have been warned that I'm not allowed to drop her off unless I have freshly-styled hair, full make-up and contact lenses, and even then, under no circumstances are her father and I to actually get out of the truck. She's granted permission for us to park well away from the coach and wave from a distance.

TUESDAY 5 AUGUST

Lulu is a dark horse. I've been worrying for weeks that she'll have no-one to sit with on the coach, and it turns out that she's had a long-standing arrangement to sit with a boy called John! She boarded the bus quite happily with $200.00 in her purse. She'll probably starve all week and come back wearing new Converse!

WEDNESDAY 6 AUGUST

Lulu rang last night to tell us that she and Lexie have had their hotel room upgraded! Apparently, the one they had been allocated only had one single bed instead of two, so they were switched to a very large, luxurious room with a fireplace, massive television and a dressing table. She was thrilled that she'll be able to do her hair and make-up in comfort.

THURSDAY 7 AUGUST

I was furious this morning to discover that Lulu has not taken her waterproof coat to Melbourne. When I texted her she pretended to be horrified that she'd 'forgotten' it, but I know that it was deliberate. I found the coat, zipped-up, on its hanger in the middle of a rack of jeans, and she NEVER hangs anything up. It was obviously a deliberate attempt at concealment. Melbourne is known as the city which can experience four seasons in one day, so if she gets rained or snowed on, it's her own fault!

The husband finished painting Lulu's room tonight. Hope she likes it.

JC is going to be weighed at the vets tomorrow. If he's lost more weight than me, I shall sulk.

FRIDAY 8 AUGUST

Went to hairdresser this morning, and am now proudly sporting a medium-length bob with a fringe! Feel about 5 years old again. (If only I could recreate that 5 year old blondeness!) The hairdresser asked me if I wanted a "POB" (Posh Spice bob) and I had to reluctantly explain that I'm far too chubby for a jaw-length hairstyle!

Spent the afternoon putting Lulu's room back together. It looks very bright and fresh after that dingy navy blue colour, and the Audrey Hepburn posters look very cool. Hope she's pleased with it.

Went to school at 4.00pm to meet the Melbourne coach, only to be told they were running 3 hours late. Eventually collected her at 7.00pm, and the poor child was absolutely exhausted. They've had very early mornings and late nights, and very busy days in-between. She got home, ate a pizza, admired her new room and climbed straight into bed. She voluntarily handed over the change from her trip, and I nearly fainted – there was over $100.00 left! I misjudged the poor girl.

Before I finish, here's the update on Jasper Conran – he has lost over 500g. I gave him a slightly larger scoop of food tonight for doing so well. He's pleased with the results, but it's been very painful for him – he still cries outside the laundry room door every evening, whimpering for extra rations!

SATURDAY 9 AUGUST

Received a letter today, explaining that we are due for our three-monthly rental inspection, and it will be carried out at 9.00am next Tuesday. Am worried sick. Need to remove all traces of Jasper Conran from the house, and make it appear as if he lives permanently outside. Am also worried because the letter states that the landlady will be present at the inspection, in addition to the rental agent. Wonder if she has her suspicions that JC lives inside. Husband thinks it's more likely that she's just being nosy and wants to look at the recent decorating. Had better start cleaning tomorrow.

SUNDAY 10 AUGUST

Nightmare day. Spent hours and hours cleaning the house. Husband went off to buy a spade, and then spent hours digging and weeding the flowerbeds and washing the guttering and windows. Don't think this house has had a proper clean for years. Will be relieved when Tuesday is over.

Went for ride in truck late afternoon. (Husband worries that I don't get out enough). Was a bit of a disaster though as my back was causing me agony after all the cleaning, so I took two painkillers and they made me drowsy. Had to keep jerking awake as felt very rude to be snoozing away while the poor husband had to keep his eyes firmly on the road.

WEEK 32
Landladies and Birthing Kits

MONDAY 11 AUGUST

Mopping, scrubbing, bleaching and polishing – another exciting day. Spent HOURS cleaning the oven and hob and re-cleaned bathroom and toilets again. House is gleaming. Have set alarm for 5.30am tomorrow morning, to get up and remove all traces of Jasper Conran. Am very nervous. Have got such a bad feeling about the landlady attending the inspection, and keep worrying that she'll come across a spare chewy bone under the dining table, or similar scenario that will give the game away.

TUESDAY 12 AUGUST

Very cross. Also very relieved. Rental Agent arrived alone and barely looked at anything – she went through the house in about 45 seconds, and didn't even look down the side of the garden where husband has toiled over the flowerbeds. I led her over to the oven and insisted she looked inside – she probably thought I was a bit crazy! I'd been up at the crack of dawn to move Jasper Conran outside. I put his wire cage in the pen and covered it with a thick rug to make it look lived-in. It obviously worked because no questions were asked about him. All in all, we passed the inspection with flying colours.

Lulu stayed at home today, due to a very bad cough and a tight chest. When I rang school to let them know she was ill, I thought I was speaking to Dame Edna when the receptionist said, "Oh, the poor little possum, you keep her snuggled up in bed today." However, the poor little possum had recovered by 10.30am, and when I asked what would make her feel better she replied, "A magazine, a sausage roll and a custard tart." Guess who trailed out to the Plaza?

WEDNESDAY 13 AUGUST

What a scary day. Was just returning from my power walk this morning when the landlady's car pulled into the driveway next door – she was going to the gym with my neighbour. We exchanged pleasantries, but I didn't linger as I was worried that Jasper would hear me talking and start barking his head off. She would have heard him because he was in his cage in the bedroom at the front of the house. I said goodbye to her and dashed indoors with a sigh of relief.

However, an hour later there was a knock on the door. I quickly shut JC in the study and answered the door. To my horror, it was my neighbour – AND THE LANDLADY! They were going for a walk and wondered if I'd like to join them. It seemed rude to say no, so I said I would love to join them if they'd just give me 5 minutes. I shut the door and rushed to put JC outside in his pen. I was a nervous wreck by the time I joined them. They were both sporting tracksuits and headbands and looked very professional, while I tagged behind in my old jeans and trainers! I wondered if they'd kindly asked me along because they thought I was lonely, or if they thought I looked fat and needed the exercise. Or maybe they thought I looked both fat AND lonely!

THURSDAY 14 AUGUST

Parent's Evening at school. Annie is in deep disgrace for only arranging appointments with two teachers. Her father says she is grounded at the weekend unless she makes some more appointments for Monday night's session. We saw the English teacher first, who praised Annie's work but then stated that she didn't feel she had Annie's full attention to the same extent that she had at the start of the year. We gave our enthusiastic permission for her to be moved to the front of the class, away from her chatty friend. Daughter is not amused.

Luckily, the maths teacher had only good things to say about both the quality of her work and her attention span. Suspect I made a bit of a faux pas though. After discussing maths, he went on to say that he would like Annie to apply for a place on the Peer Support Programme, where Year 11 pupils take responsibility for a group of Year 7s who've just moved up to middle school. I mentioned that I'd told Annie she needs these kind of activities to put on her CV when she applies for university places. He agreed with me, but then went on to stress that it's also an excellent opportunity for her to contribute to the school community. Obviously I had forgotten that the school motto is, "Enter to Learn, Go Out to Serve." Felt deeply humbled. (Ignored the husband mumbling that he makes a significant contribution via school fees!)

FRIDAY 15 AUGUST

Read an article in the Macarthur Chronicle this morning, about the Zonta Club needing volunteers at their community project tomorrow. Might go, as I really should get out a bit more. JC is becoming very clingy – perhaps we need a bit of time apart.

Out for dinner tonight to the pizza restaurant at Narellan crossroads. Lovely evening.

SATURDAY 16 AUGUST

Googled "Zonta Club" this morning. It appeared to be an upmarket WI, and its members are all professional women who hold decision-making managerial positions. Decided to go to the project.

Arrived at Appin House at 2.00pm. There were about 45 women there and we were assembling 'birthing kits' which would be distributed to poor, pregnant women who were mainly based in areas of conflict such as East Timor. The kits consisted of a black plastic sheet, swabs of gauze, three pieces of string, a scalpel, a bar of soap and a pair of silicone gloves. Felt very humble for the second time in three days. Was very sad to realise that this paltry birthing kit was all that many women would have to try and bring their babies safely into the world.

The other women were all very friendly, and I was invited to attend their next meeting and stay for dinner. Suspect they must be in dire need of foot-soldiers, as I certainly don't meet the professional requirements of Zonta membership!

PS: I had no idea that East Timor was so close to Australia – it might have affected my decision to move here if I had known we would be so close to a trouble-spot!

SUNDAY 17 AUGUST

The teenagers were in a giddy mood today. They woke me up from a very deep sleep this morning to ask me, "Who lives in Farthing Wood – is it Rupert?" I was very cross with them.

Everybody knows that Rupert lives in Nutwood.

WEEK 33
Lulu Blows a Fuse and Linda Sees a Snake

MONDAY 18 AUGUST

Parent's Evening again tonight. Both girls are back in favour. Every single one of Lulu's teachers said that she pays attention and works very hard. There are only five weeks of term left, and then they'll both move up a year and Annie will be in senior school. Where is the time going?

TUESDAY 19 AUGUST

With thoughts of rapidly ageing children and further education in mind, I spent the morning researching careers/qualifications/courses etc. on the Connexions website. When girls arrived home from school, I made them sit down and research careers with me. If you input a prospective career, it gives you all the information you could possibly need, but the naughty girls would only suggest lorry drivers and dustbin men! Gave up in frustration.

WEDNESDAY 20 AUGUST

Disaster. The ceiling lights in Lulu's bedroom packed-in on Monday and the husband was unable to sort them out. Tried swapping bulbs around, bought new bulbs, checked junction box etc. but to no avail, so I reported it to the Rental Agent but still have not heard anything. It's really getting me down now, because I'm constantly on-edge in case the landlady should knock at the door and be greeted by Jasper Conran, but also because Lulu is behaving as if her father and I have deliberately broken the lights in her room simply to cause her maximum inconvenience, purely for our own amusement! It is annoying though – she has to get dressed in the study each morning, and cannot see in her room after 6.00pm each night.

THURSDAY 21 AUGUST

Called at Rental Agent today to enquire if they'd heard from the landlady. It turns out they've been trying to speak to her for days, but she never returns their calls. In desperation, they have hand-delivered a letter asking her to ring them urgently regarding repairs. We've reported three problems now without any response, so this evening we went late-night shopping and bought Lulu a lamp from Target in the hope of de-fusing her irritable mood.

FRIDAY 22 AUGUST

Jasper Conran is such a star. He's been weighed at the vet again and has lost over a kilo. He now weighs 8.380kg and has lost more than 10% of his bodyweight. If he'd joined Weight Watchers he'd have been presented with an award by now. And would have been clapped vigorously by all the members.

SATURDAY 23 AUGUST

Had a long lie-in this morning (possibly connected to bottle of Jacob's Creek sparkling chardonnay which was consumed last night – delicious). Husband completed some work admin on laptop then chauffeured Annie to meet friends. Lulu stayed in reading new book. Very quiet day.

SUNDAY 24 AUGUST

Scary, scary day. Drove to Coogee, which is just down the coast from Bondi and very cool. Lulu announced she'd be happy to stay in Sydney forever if we bought a house there. So would we, Lulu, so would we.

After a short stop at Coogee, we drove down the coast, past all the beautiful scenic beaches, toward Botany Bay. On the way, we stopped for ice-creams at a tourist spot near a museum. We noticed a crowd gathered around a fenced-off area across from the car park, and jokingly said that it must be cane toad racing or something similar. Anyway, I sauntered over while casually eating my chocolate sundae. Almost screamed in horror. It was a reptile demonstration and, as I nudged my way to the front, a Steve Irwin-type man was just getting a red-bellied black snake out of a hessian sack – ABOUT A METRE AWAY FROM MY FACE!!! And there were other sacks on the ground, still tied up, and goodness only knows what was in those – probably deadly brown snakes, knowing these strange reptile people!

I dashed back to the truck and locked the doors. I thought I'd become quite complacent about snakes, having read in the newspaper so many reports of them invading houses, sports centres, outdoor loos etc. but I hadn't realised quite how BIG they are. The one he was holding was massive.

When I went to bed tonight, I slept with the quilt right over my head – it was a bit warm, but better warm than terrified!

WEEK 34
Good Wife, Bad Wife

MONDAY 25 AUGUST

Have calmed down after yesterday's slippery reptile encounter. Rental Agent rang to say that our landlady had finally given permission for Lulu's bedroom lights to be fixed, and by 11.30am the electrician had been and fixed the problem. The whole job only took him about 15 minutes, yet we've had to pay out $40.00 for a lamp and put up with the inconvenience (and teenage stroppiness) for a week. The whole rental issue is starting to really get me down, especially since the shower head has now started shooting off if you turn the shower on too fast!

TUESDAY 26 AUGUST

I have to admit there are times when being a Very Good Wife can be terribly boring. Take today for instance – I was up at 6.00am to prise the teenagers from their beds, made breakfast and lunches, loaded the washing machine, cleaned the bathroom, swept the hall floor, emptied the rubbish bins, ironed six work shirts for the husband, walked the dog and pegged out the laundry, and it was still only 8.55am!

Sometimes I think fondly of the UK days when my inner Bad Wife would come to the fore and I'd catch the bus into the city and while away a few hours in Harvey Nichols, admiring the Alice Temperley dresses and designer handbags, and possibly squirrelling away a small purchase from the Nars stand at Space NK. I'd have lunch at Bagel Nash (smoked salmon bagel) and wander down to Links of London to plan my fantasy charm bracelet, before buying a little chocolate treat from Charbonnel et Walker and a magazine from W H Smith to see me through the journey home. Since we've been in Aus, I've been too good for too long – think I need to rebel a little.

(Re the Nars make-up – I find that if you put your new purchase IMMEDIATELY into your cosmetic bag, it looks as if it's always been there and therefore minimises any guilt you might feel at spending good money on yet another taupe eyeshadow).

WEDNESDAY 27 AUGUST

The husband is yet again tripping off to Melbourne, this time for three days, so have washed and ironed almost every single shirt he owns. Decided that if I'm going to rebel, then I'd better get the house in order first, so that I can play truant with a clear conscience. Think I'll plan a whole day of lunch and shopping in one of the exclusive bays around the city, and maybe have a manicure and pedicure at an express nail bar – I definitely deserve it.

THURSDAY 28 AUGUST

Husband was up at 4.00am this morning to catch his flight to Melbourne. Felt a bit guilty because I never heard him go, and so never actually said goodbye. I didn't want him to go because Qantas airlines have been in the news recently, after allegedly having some very near disasters. I like my family to be safely on the ground.

Early night tonight, after researching where to go for my day out, along with the relevant train schedules. Have narrowed it down to Bondi, Double Bay or Paddington.

FRIDAY 29 AUGUST

Disastrous day. Lulu came home and confessed that she lost her glasses over a week ago. She remembers having them in the history lesson last Friday, but can't recall seeing them since. I rang school immediately, but they haven't been handed in. I remained calm, but am actually furious. And suspicious. It's very odd that she's suddenly 'lost' them after asking me for the last two months if she can have some new ones. Bang goes my rebellious shopping spree. Damn teenagers. I've warned her that I can only afford the most basic, cheapest pair.

SATURDAY 30 AUGUST

Took Lulu for eyes testing - $65.00. Cheapest pair of glasses we could find were over $240.00 and were quite hideous. Couldn't face arguing with her, so sent her off with friends (who were 'helping' her choose some frames) and decided to go back tomorrow.

Husband returned from Melbourne at 1.30pm with the obligatory severe 'business tension headache,' ie, a thumping hangover. Was very dismayed when he collapsed on sofa, because I was desperately bored and wanted to go out. I knew he was tired though, so I didn't complain. However, he must have sensed I was a bit fed-up (maybe he heard me sighing) because he took me out 'roo-spotting! We drove through Cobbitty and out into the countryside. We saw lots of kangaroos – big ones, little ones, young ones, old ones and even mums with babies in their pouch. They are so sweet close-up. Their upper bodies and heads are very tiny and delicate, yet their back legs and tails are huge. I wonder if the warmer weather is bringing them out, as we haven't seen any at all and then suddenly there are whole herds of them everywhere.

SUNDAY 31 AUGUST

Damn those teenagers. Guess who came out of the optician with a huge grin after watching her mother order her a pair of Dolce &

Gabbana spectacles? That's right, the youngest teenager. When it came down to it, there wasn't that much difference in price between the hideous specs and the designer ones, so it just wasn't worth the sulking and I caved-in. I know I'm a soft-touch, but I did draw the line at the Mui Mui glasses – I'm not quite THAT soft.

Persuaded husband to drop me at Macarthur Square as girls were busy with homework assignments and revising, and he had some trashy Chevy Chase film lined-up. It's not quite Double Bay, but at least it's an afternoon out. Didn't have much cash-flow after paying Messrs Dolce and Gabbana for their superior design skills, so decided to go to cinema as it was only $15.00. Watched Baby Mama and had a lovely time – just me, the film and a very large Diet Coke with ice. My inner Bad Wife is obviously very tame these days, perhaps I need a little more practice at releasing her. Came home and painted nails myself with Estee Lauder's 'White Beige.' One of these days I will actually get to that beauty salon – probably when I'm 80 and hobbling there with a zimmer frame!

WEEK 35
Striving for Excellence – Yet Again!

MONDAY 1 SEPTEMBER

I have SO neglected my self-improvement programme. This house is just so unglamorous that I don't feel compelled to live up to my surroundings any more, and am letting myself go to seed. Need to get a very firm grip. Am still far too fat for my sunhat.

TUESDAY 2 SEPTEMBER

Decided to start with the basics today, so removed all nail polish from fingers and toes and got the shock of my life – I have got the toe nails of a 90 year old! I have worn polish on my toenails ever since we arrived here; I've never really taken it off, just kept topping it up. When I finally took it all off, I discovered my toe nails were yellow! A quick Google informed me that, apparently, this happens when your nails never get a chance to 'breathe.' Rushed down to chemist in the Plaza to buy some basecoat to protect them in future. Also in chemist was some special lotion to lighten discoloured toenails, but did not purchase as was very expensive. However, when I got home I mixed my own little remedy (bleach and water) and that worked a treat – perhaps I should market it. My toes are back to being 43 years old again, thank goodness. Applied a very thick layer of basecoat before I painted them. Don't ever want 90 year old toes again – except, obviously, when am actually 90.

WEDNESDAY 3 SEPTEMBER

Apparently, my husband worries about me. He thinks that Jasper Conran and I spend far too much time on our own. Haven't told him that we just LOVE the peace and quiet (which is actually a euphemism for 'endless naps'). Anyway, he asked if we wanted to go to work with him today, so we said yes – and what an eye-opener that was. He has the life of Reilly. He rides around in his 4x4 all day, and pulls up in some glamorous little bay to eat his lunch. Sometimes he has lunch out. We pulled-up at a very chic new development called Breakfast Point. It was divine. Very Cape Cod. Had a look on the website when I got home and saw that the apartments on the waterfront start at $1.3m – which means that WE won't be moving there. Had a great day out, but Jasper and I were flagging a bit by mid-afternoon as we missed our daily snooze!

THURSDAY 4 SEPTEMBER

Purely in the name of research, seeing as I've taken up my campaign to become elegant and ladylike again, I bought Australian Vogue magazine today. As luck would have it, there was an article entitled, "DO-IT-YOURSELF – BE A LADY." It explains that you should, "Go for demure looks, set off with dainty details," and it shows pictures of very elegant dresses, shoes, handbags, gloves and brooches. Unfortunately, though, they're all by designers such as Alexander McQueen, Roland Mouret, Lanvin, Marni, Chanel and Tiffany. In other words, they're all way out of my price league. Also, although they were all very elegant, they were actually rather impractical for hanging around Harrington Park – I don't think the pencil skirts and high heels would be conducive to striding around the lake and bending down to pick up dog poop! Must not be deterred though. Must strive, strive, strive to be more sophisticated.

FRIDAY 5 SEPTEMBER

The girls completed a sponsored walk at school last week, in aid of disadvantaged children at a school in Tanzania, and they had to take their sponsor money in today. They were each expected to raise $40.00, but there was no-one except me to sponsor them. Didn't feel we could ask the neighbours, as the people on our left are retired and the ones on our right are students. Felt very mean when I was grumpy at having to hand over the money this morning – I must not begrudge money for the poor children when I've just spent $400.00 on Lulu's new glasses!

SATURDAY 6 SEPTEMBER

Huge row with Lulu today. We were going shopping and her father decided to tease her – it was raining heavily and he wouldn't open the car doors to let her in. When she did get in, she was absolutely furious and thumped him hard on the shoulder. He was in agony. I was so angry with her, I was almost beyond words. I just opened the car door and sent her back inside, so she missed her afternoon out. Gave the husband a very stern talking-to. Everybody knows that you should NEVER mess with a teenage girl's hair, especially after they've just spent over an hour washing, drying and straightening it.

SUNDAY 7 SEPTEMBER

It's Father's Day today, and what a lovely day we've had. Girls bought their dad a John Wayne dvd, a chocolate orange and some Cadbury's Roses. Jasper Conran bought him a very sweet card.

We went to the Northern Beaches this afternoon. It was a bit of a fraught journey because we almost ended up in the Lane Cove Tunnel, and this is NOT where you want to be if you're claustrophobic. I kept clutching my head in panic and the naughty girls were laughing hysterically in the back seat. Anyway, clever old husband managed to avoid the tunnel and we had a great time browsing the chic boutiques and gift shops. (Strictly speaking, girls and I had a great time browsing – husband and Jasper waited outside, as usual).

When we got home I made a delicious roast chicken dinner with Yorkshire puddings, baby roast potatoes, sweetcorn, carrots and cauliflower cheese. We all enjoyed dinner and then collapsed in front of Criminal Minds then CSI Miami, while gathering our strength to face yet another busy week. (Strictly speaking yet again, girls and husband will have another busy week, Jasper and I will take it quite easy, as usual)!

WEEK 36
Into the Stratosphere

MONDAY 8 SEPTEMBER

Grazia magazine has just launched in Australia, and I read some of it on the internet. There was a very interesting paragraph re 'Alpha Females' which explained how these superior beings can seduce and shine way beyond their 'stratosphere' and how these cool people cast a net of intrigue around their group. I want to be stratospherically gorgeous. And cool. And seductive. And stylish. And intriguing. Have retrieved the ankle weights from the back of my wardrobe and am going out walking.

TUESDAY 9 SEPTEMBER

Sometimes, my ability to wheedle my way around my husband amazes even me – even though I've been doing it for 22 years! Somehow, tonight I persuaded him to take me to Borders so that I could buy Harper's Bazaar. Felt in dire need of some international glamour, and Harper's never disappoints. Plan backfired a bit though, because one of the articles left me a bit depressed – "What do your clothes say about you?" by Rita Wilson. Have realised that my clothes say I'm spending far too much time out here in the countryside and not enough time in the chic inner-city.

WEDNESDAY 10 SEPTEMBER

Have been for consultation with neurosurgeon today, to discuss MRI scan results. She patiently explained the operational procedure to me in great detail, and I patiently explained to her in great detail that I do not want to have an operation. She agreed that we can just monitor the situation for the moment, but if the pain returns then I must go straight back to see her again. Her parting shot was that losing weight would definitely ease the situation and relieve pressure on my spine. My parting shot (spoken only in my head) was that the situation has placed great pressure on my bank account. It has cost over $300.00 for two consultations, and only half of that can be claimed back through Medicare. It would appear that the 'reciprocal healthcare arrangements' with the UK are not quite as reciprocal as the immigration lawyers led us to believe!

Still, money worries aside, I've now got even more impetus to stick to my diet. If all goes to plan, I should be stratospherically gorgeous by the end of the year.

THURSDAY 11 SEPTEMBER

I cannot believe what I am hearing. This is just my rotten luck. Read on the internet news today that some eminent scientists in Europe spent yesterday trying to recreate the Big Bang, and if they succeed there is a chance that the earth will implode and disappear down a Black Hole!

It's not fair – just as I make plans to be stratospherically gorgeous, the stratosphere is about to be blasted out of existence. And apparently, it won't happen immediately, but in about four years' time. My Worry List was practically empty, seeing as the threat of an immediate operation has lifted, and now it will be full to capacity for the next four years. I really must try to keep up more with important world events, instead of reading about them after they've happened.

FRIDAY 12 SEPTEMBER

Lulu has a friend staying over tonight, and they're going to a party together tomorrow afternoon. Hilary is a pretty, petite girl who lives a few miles from us in a very rural area. I was quizzing her about snakes, and wished I hadn't once I'd heard the answer. Apparently, they get lots of snakes around their house, and her dad always keeps a shovel handy so he can chop off their heads! When Hilary was a baby, her mum found a snake curled up among the clothes in the ironing basket! Spent the evening thinking up excuses in case Lulu receives a return invitation.

SATURDAY 13 SEPTEMBER

Girls were up early and off to the hairdresser, then disappeared into Narellan. They re-appeared a few hours later with Lulu sporting a very chic fringed hairstyle and carrying a tank containing a blue fighting fish named Hamilton! The pet shop has sold them a tank which is far too small, so I will have to buy a larger one as I can't bear to think of the poor little thing being unhappy. At least there's no danger of this pet getting us evicted.

SUNDAY 14 SEPTEMBER

Quiet day. Absolutely pouring with rain. Girls revising for exams so husband, Jasper and I decided to go out for a drive, despite the weather. We headed for a lookout point at the foot of the Blue Mountains.

We were very hungry so stopped at a petrol station and bought a few (extortionately priced) snacks and drinks, which we ate in the dreary car park. Decided to turn back home as rain was becoming torrential. As we pulled out of the car park, we spotted a rather nice patisserie with a large undercover area where we could have had a more substantial lunch – was very cross.

On the way home we called at pet shop and bought a larger tank for Hamilton ($30.00). The damn fish has cost $65.00 in total – I could have had my hair done for that. Or bought a new Chanel nail polish and still had some change.

WEEK 37
Snakes in the Grass?

MONDAY 15 SEPTEMBER

I'm having serious issues with the Australian wildlife at the moment. Summer seems to be bringing them all to the fore.

Kangaroos – just as I've taken the hoppitty beasts to heart, I heard on the news that a kangaroo has attacked a jogger in Melbourne. I suspect that the cute 'roos we spot on our country drives are just mums and toddlers, and the big daddies are keeping watch from the trees.

Snakes – my neighbour was telling me she saw a deadly brown snake in her garden last summer. She thinks it was looking for water, as we are surrounded by swimming pools. She also told me that her sister had a snake sneak into her house, and how a neighbour's dog was bitten a few years ago. Have stopped leaving the screen door open for Jasper Conran to stroll in and out. It's kept firmly shut now. And securely locked. And tightly bolted.

Lizards – bent down this morning to scoop up JC's poopy, and almost picked up a lizard which was camouflaged in the bark chippings. It scuttled off when my hand touched it. I jumped a mile. And screamed a little. Luckily, my hand was encased in a green poopy bag.

Despite my aversion to the wildlife, I've entered a competition in the Macarthur Chronicle to have 'Breakfast with the Koalas' at Sydney Wildlife World. Hope they don't feed us eucalyptus leaves if we win!

TUESDAY 16 SEPTEMBER

Lulu seems to be settling into life here at last. She keeps 'phoning me from the school bus, asking if she can meet her friends in Narellan after school. What she actually means is, can she rush home, get changed, relieve me of at least $10.00 and go and meet her friends in town to squander some cash together. My cash. (Well, strictly speaking, it's the husband's cash).

Tonight though, she came home with a different request – could she go to Hilary's house at the weekend to ride Hilary's horses with her? Oh no, this is my worst nightmare. Yes, of course I'll be happy for her to go and hang about in a snake-infested paddock, riding horses of unknown (to me) temperament. At least the four years of extortionately-priced riding lessons during her early childhood should stand her in good stead.

WEDNESDAY 17 SEPTEMBER

Happy birthday to me! Was woken up by the teenagers and Jasper Conran holding cards and present (note the singular tense). Husband is away in Canberra (grumble, grumble) but he rang to say hello. Girls left to catch school bus at 7.10am and I sat down to plan a self-indulgent day as birthday treat to myself. This was actually much more difficult than it sounds, as ALL my days are so self-indulgent that coming up with something different was quite a challenge! In the end, Jasper and I settled for eating a box of Belgian chocolates while watching The Nanny Diaries dvd (present from girls). Had a lovely time, but this was over and done with by 10.45am so went to Plaza and bought a couple of magazines with which to while away the afternoon. JC and I sat outside in the sunshine with a packet of Doritos and a glass of Diet Coke. Girls were home at 3.00pm and I made them roast chicken, but I had a much later meal of smoked salmon and king prawns – another little birthday treat!

THURSDAY 18 SEPTEMBER

Am in agony with toothache. Have been suffering very mildly for over a week, but today is unbearable. Am terrified of going to dentist (good old claustrophobia again). Finally plucked up courage to go and make an appointment, and the kind receptionist fitted me in immediately! This would be unheard of in the UK. Was very pleased as it meant that I had no opportunity to work myself up into a blind panic. However, dentist could find nothing wrong, and took a very expensive x-ray to make sure. Came out relieved, but also $145.00 poorer. Bang goes my birthday treat from the husband when we go shopping at the weekend.

FRIDAY 19 SEPTEMBER

Have today spent 3 hours at the hairdresser having my frizzy mop highlighted, cut and blow-dried, courtesy of the birthday money from my dear mother-in-law, and it's cheered me up a treat after the dental fiasco.

Took girls to the movies tonight to see 'Angus, Thongs and Perfect Snogging.' Enjoyed it, but quite disconcerted to see how much time teenage girls spend obsessing about boys and kissing. The husband says he prefers to think that they just shake hands and say goodbye. He's only just come to terms with today's teenage hugging phenomenon.

SATURDAY 20 SEPTEMBER

Scary, scary day. Have been lost in the countryside with only 40 minutes until nightfall, and witnessed a bushfire just metres away from the truck. Am too overwrought to write tonight. Will fill in diary tomorrow.

SUNDAY 21 SEPTEMBER

Here's the full account of yesterday's trip.

Girls were out and about with various friends, so husband, dog and I set off for scenic drive down the coast. Called at Wollongong, Shellharbour and Kiama, before setting off back through the countryside via Kangaroo Valley and Sheepwash Road (I swear I'm not making these names up). Remained calm during the drive along scary mountain road, and breathed sigh of relief as we levelled out at top of mountain. Played my new 'Jackie Album' cd (birthday present from lovely friend) so we listened to David Cassidy, The Bay City Rollers, Paper Lace etc. (Must confess to sniggering a little when husband knew all the words to 'Have You Seen Her' by the Chi-Lites)!

Anyway, was enjoying peaceful drive when husband suddenly announced that we were lost. The SatNav had blown a bit of a fuse and sent us well off the beaten track. As we looked around, as far as the eye could see, everything was flat scrubland and the SatNav was refusing to show us the main road. And there was no signal on the mobile. It was only 40 minutes until darkness and I was terrified. Husband was comforted that a lone car had been following us for miles, so we weren't entirely alone, but I was worried that it contained a murdering madman.

Was petrified we'd be stuck in the wilderness in the pitch black, being assailed by bounding kangaroos and psychopathic murderers, but while I was shaking with fear, the husband was humming, "Billy, Don't Be A Hero!"

Thankfully, after half an hour of panic, the main road appeared on the SatNav screen and we managed to get back to civilisation. However, we'd only been on the main road for a few minutes when we spotted billowing smoke ahead. It turned out there was a bushfire along the side of the motorway, but luckily it wasn't on our side of the carriageway. Big, hunky firemen were dealing with the flames as we passed, and we didn't hang around to watch.

Arrived home to find a message from Lulu saying that she was tucked up safely, watching dvds at Hilary's, and hadn't encountered any snakes. Thank the Lord we're all safe and sound. Australia is playing havoc with my nerves!

WEEK 38
Goal!

MONDAY 22 SEPTEMBER

Have been wracked with my recurring dental pain all weekend, and I think I've realised what the problem is – stress. Very often over the last few weeks I've suddenly realised that I'm clenching my jaw very tightly, and have to consciously force myself to relax it. I know it sounds incredulous to say that I'm suffering from stress, considering my current indolent lifestyle, but I haven't told you about my other Worry List – the unofficial one.

The Official Worry List has only two issues – bird flu and black holes – but the unofficial one contains HUGE unresolved issues which I can't do anything about, such as our inability to sell the house back home and the fact that it has drastically fallen in value due to the global financial crash, the precarious and expensive medical situation here and the whole issue of girls going to university and the overseas student university fees.

Desperately need to stop worrying before I wear away my jaw – a lop-sided John Merrick face would not be very elegant. It's a pity I didn't realise what the problem was BEFORE I had a very expensive dental x-ray last week!

TUESDAY 23 SEPTEMBER

A new Starbucks-type café has opened at the Plaza and I arranged to meet Rebecca there for lunch today. I spent ages getting ready;

wore my jeans, a black t-shirt, best jewellery etc. and washed and straightened my hair into frizz-free submission. I painted my fingers and toes and applied fresh make-up. Was half-way to Plaza, feeling very pleased with the finished result, when I tripped down the kerb and snapped the toe-strap on my chic jewelled sandals. Didn't have time to go back and change, so had to sort of hop and limp the rest of the way. Rebecca just thought it was my back/leg playing-up again, so I didn't enlighten her. Had a nice time, but was depressed to realise that elegance had eluded me once more. Perhaps I should just give up now and accept that I'll never be ladylike.

WEDNESDAY 24 SEPTEMBER

No – I cannot give up. The chic Sydney girl is still rattling at my ribcage (through all the padding, naturally) and I can't abandon her just yet. Went for a long walk with Mr Conran this morning, as he's due to be weighed on Friday and I'm hoping he'll be under 8kg. I won't be defeated by a weakened shoe strap.

FRIDAY 26 SEPTEMBER

Jasper Conran has reached his goal weight! He is under 8kg! 7.890kg to be exact. He is such a good boy. Why do I not possess the same willpower?

SATURDAY 27 SEPTEMBER

I really must remember that Jasper Conran did not actually possess any willpower. It was a higher power (me) that took control of his diet, issued him with very meagre rations and kept temptation firmly under lock and key outside of mealtimes. If only someone would do the same to me.

SUNDAY 28 SEPTEMBER

The husband has decreed that we need to get out and exercise more, instead of merely driving around sightseeing at weekends. He intends to begin this regime next weekend. Feeling very apprehensive, as husband does not possess my fickle personality, and fear he will be planning exhaustive route marches.

WEEK 39
A Chic Sydney Girl at Last!

MONDAY 29 SEPTEMBER

There IS a chic Sydney girl in this family after all, but I'm sorry to tell you that her name is not Linda – it's Lulu!

Lulu has been into the city today with her friend, Hilary. She was wearing very tight skinny jeans, black camisole, black cardigan, silver ballet shoes and MY BLACK SUEDE KELLY BAG! She'd been up since 5.00am and spent an hour straightening her hair – I could smell the singed tresses as I kissed her goodbye. Despite having no spare cash, I somehow rustled up $50.00 for her to go shopping with. Her lift arrived at 7.00am and as I peeped through the shutters to watch her go, I'm sure I felt the ground shift beneath me. How come I'm stuck at home in baggy pyjamas, sporting frizzy bed-head hair, while my youngest child is out living it up in the city, looking like a supermodel?

TUESDAY 30 SEPTEMBER

Lulu arrived home safe and sound at 7.00pm yesterday. As it was raining she'd had to buy a small umbrella and guess what – she sacrificed her hairstyle to keep my Kelly bag dry! At least she has her priorities straight – she can always re-style her hair, but there's no money for new Kelly bags at the moment. (My conscience is making me point out that it's not actually a genuine Hermes Kelly bag, but was still very expensive and is chic and irreplaceable).

WEDNESDAY 1 OCTOBER

Enough is enough. It's now too hot to tolerate Jasper Conran in my bed any longer. Tonight I tied him to the bedside cabinet and made him sleep in his basket. He sulked a bit, but took it in good grace.

However, the husband thought that this was his cue to stray into my side of the bed. I woke up and he was spread-eagled like a starfish, while I perched on the edge. I sent him back again and remained on Border Patrol all night. I've just ejected one doe-eyed, furry creature from my sleeping space, and I certainly don't need another one filling it up again!

THURSDAY 2 OCTOBER

Am very scared. Went to supermarket this afternoon, and as I picked up an onion something shot into my finger. Managed to remove splinter when I got home, but now fingertip has gone white and is throbbing off. Am afraid something might have bitten me, and the 'splinter' is actually poison. This damn country. Everywhere you turn there are scary, deadly beasts.

A man was eaten by crocodiles in North Queensland this week. It's very sad, of course, but I don't understand why anyone would go camping near a croc-infested river. Apparently, it got him when he went to check his crab nets, and all his wife found was a snapped rope and crocodile 'slide marks' on the riverbank. There are no wild crocs in NSW, but it still makes me very jittery!

FRIDAY 3 OCTOBER

Lulu has decided upon her future career – she wants to be the next Stella McCartney (minus the shiny forehead, naturally). With this in mind, I took her shopping today and let her choose a dress pattern and some material. With such lofty aspirations, I thought she really ought to get some practical experience. Let's see if she still wants to be a dress designer once she's grappled with sewing machines, zips and iron-on interfacing!

SATURDAY 4 OCTOBER

Yet another disaster. This morning the husband reiterated his decree that we can no longer idle our weekends away driving aimlessly around the countryside, and declared that he was going to accompany me on a power walking session around the lake. We left the teenagers asleep, and Jasper Conran crying in his basket, and set off at marching pace. I was puffing and panting after only 2 minutes, but daren't complain. We rounded the top of the lake and passed the children's playground, but as we neared the jetty I slipped on a rock which had fallen onto the path, and crashed onto the banking. I screamed a little (quite a lot, actually) as I was laid out in the long scrubby grass and felt sure there would a snake lurking nearby. A crowd of joggers came dashing over to help, as the husband grabbed my hand and hauled me to my feet. My left ankle was in agony and I could barely put any weight on it. The husband left me on the path and went to fetch the truck. By this time, the crowd of joggers was joined by a group of toddlers and their mothers, and an old lady in a wheelchair, plus her carer. Was very relieved when the husband arrived back with the truck and I was able to thank the (really quite large) crowd for their concern, and limp to the truck, supported by the husband.

Arrived home and collapsed upon sofa, while husband filled a bucket with ice-cold water to soak the injured ankle. Remained upon sofa all afternoon, being waited upon by concerned family and fussed over by faithful dog. Tried to stand up at dinner time, and almost fainted. It would appear that the tumble has upset my delicate spinal discs again, in addition to injuring ankle. Managed to limp to bathroom, then collapsed into bed.

SUNDAY 5 OCTOBER

In far too much pain to write diary. Will have to take a break next week. Will have no news to record anyway, as confined to bed and sofa.

WEEK 41
House Arrest

MONDAY 13 OCTOBER

Still in dire pain and confined to house. Feeling very guilty for making minimal effort re Annie's birthday last Friday, but her father compensated by throwing money at the problem. It would appear that a boyfriend is on the scene (and has been for some time, according to her sister), so the husband ferried them to Macarthur Square for trip to cinema and pizza restaurant, then collected them again. Husband informs me the boyfriend, Damian, is very polite.

TUESDAY 14 OCTOBER

Husband has requested house visit from GP. Not sure if we have to pay for this or not!

WEDNESDAY 15 OCTOBER

After thoroughly twisting and turning ankle, doctor decreed that ankle must be rested for one more week then daily walking must begin in earnest. If back seizes up any further, I'll be in dire trouble. Am apparently on verge of being a hospital case.

THURSDAY 16 OCTOBER

Rebecca very kindly rang me today. She had heard about my accident on the grapevine (hopefully via school network, and not from the random crowd at the lake) and offered to help with housework, shopping etc. I declined her offer, but invited her round for coffee tomorrow.

FRIDAY 17 OCTOBER

Rebecca brought doughnuts! It would have been very rude to throw kindness in her face by not eating them. Unfortunately, my exercise routine has been well and truly scuppered by the husband's disastrous fitness plans, and my well-intentioned dietary aspirations appear to have been scuppered along with them. Must focus, despite blinding pain.

SUNDAY 19 OCTOBER

Tried to stand on the bathroom scales this morning. Luckily, could not balance on poorly ankle long enough for needle to settle in a straight line. Dare not think about what I must weigh after two weeks' convalescence.

WEEK 42
Apple Pies

MONDAY 20 OCTOBER

Have very gingerly been outside the house today. Walked down to the Plaza and back again. Did not take Jasper Conran as could not cope with bending down to pick up poopy, or with him pulling on the lead when he (very rarely) has a spurt of energy. Ankle feeling much better, but back still very painful.

TUESDAY 21 OCTOBER

Woke up feeling much brighter, and managed to circuit the entire lake, albeit very slowly.

WEDNESDAY 22 OCTOBER

Feeling so pleased with self for managing to get moving again, that decided to call in at the Plaza take-away and buy BBQ chicken for lunch. Shop is owned by very nice elderly Italian gentleman named Toni, who was interested in how we came to live on Harrington Park and what the husband does for a living. I found the second question quite hard to answer (the husband appears to drive around construction sites and architect's offices, introducing everyone to Polyplas pte and persuading them all to use Gripples in their construction projects) but did my best. He appeared to be impressed. I shall take Jasper Conran to meet him once I feel up to it.

FRIDAY 23 OCTOBER

The recent set-back means I am, of course, still too fat for my sunhat, and the sunny weather has brought my old furrowed brow problem to the fore once more. Need to investigate sunglasses. Definitely deserve a treat after all this pain.

SATURDAY 24 OCTOBER

Husband dropped me in Camden to look for some new trainers. Sadly, the only trainers within my budget were in a cut-price shop and were a brand named "Apple Pie!" The daughters will disown me, yet again.

SUNDAY 26 OCTOBER

Realised with a start that our rental agreement is due to end in one week, yet no-one at the agency has mentioned this. Husband insisted on taking me out for Sunday drive and lunch at Dee Why beach. Enjoyed Croque Monsieur and ice-cold Diet Coke, but unable to relax due to worry over rental agreement. Will limp to Plaza first thing tomorrow morning and consult the agent.

WEEK 43
Busted!

MONDAY 27 OCTOBER

Limped to Plaza and was on Rental Agent's doorstep when shop opened. It appeared they had been expecting me some time ago. I explained that recent accident and subsequent pain had resulted in important issues slipping my mind. Agent was very sympathetic, but nonetheless had to explain that the landlady has decided to put the rental house up for sale. She would like us to stay on as long as possible with no signed agreement in place. In effect, this means she can throw us out with literally no notice!

Dashed home (as fast as limping leg would carry me) and telephoned the husband to relay latest disaster.

TUESDAY 28 OCTOBER

The husband has decreed that we must begin looking for another rental property immediately. The lease expires on Saturday, and that leaves us in a very precarious position. We are very foolish to have allowed this to happen, but the husband is extremely busy with work and, being so poorly, the renewal date had simply slipped my mind.

WEDNESDAY 29 OCTOBER

Oh dear. Today there was a knock on the door and I blithely answered it without first putting Mr Conran outside in his pen. Unfortunately, it was the landlady, who had come round to explain the position re termination of lease. Jasper was very pleased to welcome our visitor, and he skipped around in delight before jumping up onto her knee and licking her face. I tried to catch him, but he eluded me a couple of times before I finally managed to push him out of the patio doors and into his pen. I innocently ignored the elephant in the room (dog in the pen) and gave the landlady my full attention. Luckily, she had come to grovel slightly. It would appear that the landlady and her husband have reassessed their financial priorities and no longer wish to keep this rental house. They intend to sell as soon as possible, and a For Sale sign will be erected tomorrow. However, in the meantime, they would like us to stay on for as long as possible, on a week by week basis. They obviously would like our rental money, and might find it difficult to attract another tenant with the house being up for sale. They obviously also want to have their cake and eat it too. I was extremely polite to the landlady, but intend to begin searching for another property immediately.

THURSDAY 30 OCTOBER

The problem I've got is this: The rental agent we are currently using is the only one at the Plaza. If I approach them re other houses to rent, will they inform the landlady? They obviously won't want to lose our income either. Will let the husband decide what to do. Feel very stressed. Is impossible situation.

FRIDAY 31 OCTOBER

Husband and I drove into Narellan late this afternoon, to visit rental agents in effort to find another property. Very worried. There does not appear to be many properties on the market at the moment. Do not want to move from Harrington Park when girls are finally feeling more settled in this area.

There was one large house on Harrington Park available, although it was much more expensive than the Doll's House. Have arranged to see it on Monday evening.

SATURDAY 1 NOVEMBER

Too depressed to do much today. Made huge effort to present cheerful face to the teenagers. Do not wish to worry them when they have exams looming.

SUNDAY 2 NOVEMBER

Very quiet day. Supervised the teenagers' revision schedule, and supplied them with ice-cream sundaes as reward for hard work.

Fingers crossed the house viewing is successful tomorrow.

WEEK 44
Race Day

MONDAY 3 NOVEMBER

Such a stroke of luck today. I called in at Italian Toni's take-away this lunchtime, and happened to relay our latest woes to him. It turns out that he actually OWNS the house we are going to see this afternoon!!! He asked after the husband's visa and when I explained that it was a 457 visa (which means a more-or-less guaranteed income) he said we can rent his house. He will ring the rental agent in Narellan and instruct them to rent it to us, no matter who else turns up to view. We viewed the house at 4.30pm, and sealed the deal with the agent. Only one other person turned up, and it would appear that their income was not as secure as ours anyway. We are to pay a deposit on Wednesday to seal the deal.

TUESDAY 4 NOVEMBER

Melbourne Cup day. Husband is sulking because he's not going this year. It's too expensive to take customers from NSW, considering all the flights and hotels, so his boss has suggested they do a later hospitality event here on the doorstep. I, however, had a great Melbourne Cup day. My lovely neighbour, Noeline, invited me round for lunch and to watch the race. We enjoyed cheese, salami, grapes, strawberries, crackers, taramasalata, olives, carrots and huge glasses of chilled white wine. We lounged in comfy chairs, eating, drinking and watching the racing while the pool sparkled behind us!

WEDNESDAY 5 NOVEMBER

Went to Narellan to pay deposit on new rental property. Am deeply depressed at thought of packing up and moving yet again. Three different houses in 11 months does not make for a settled life.

THURSDAY 6 NOVEMBER

The husband is away yet again. This time he's out in the city with some UK friends who are here on the rugby tour. His boss told him to book a room on the company credit card and enjoy himself! Who's going to finance a night out for me, that's what I'd like to know!

SATURDAY 8 NOVEMBER

Went to Cronulla this afternoon with Annie and Damian. Left the teenagers to wander by themselves while husband and I sat on the terrace of a very busy bar drinking pina coladas (me) and low-alcohol beer (him) while reading Harper's Bazaar (me) and the Sydney Daily Telegraph (him). Met up with the teenagers again at 6.00pm for dinner at Nulla Nulla, a cool restaurant in the town centre. Husband says that the bar we were in earlier is the one where the Cronulla Sharks rugby players go to party on a Saturday night! Thank goodness we left before dark!

SUNDAY 9 NOVEMBER

When I was chatting with the rental agent a few days ago, she relayed the story of her nephew who had experienced spinal problems similar to mine. Apparently, he visited a local chiropractor who had him on his feet again in no time. Intend to ring this place tomorrow and arrange appointment for as soon as possible.

WEEK 45
Life Thru a (Broken) Lens

MONDAY 10 NOVEMBER

I answered a knock on the door this morning to discover a very sheepish-looking landlady requesting an appointment to bring a potential buyer to view the property. Agreed upon Wednesday at 11.00am which will give me enough time to tidy round after family leave for work and school.

TUESDAY 11 NOVEMBER

Feeling so much better. Sprained ankle is back to normal, and dodgy discs more or less behaving.

WEDNESDAY 12 NOVEMBER

Very cross with Annie. She has broken her glasses and has an important exam at school tomorrow. Husband called at Plaza on way home and purchased Superglue, but they have snapped right across the bridge and are impossible to glue back together.

THURSDAY 13 NOVEMBER

Huge row this morning, when I decreed that Lulu must lend her sister the Dolce & Gabbana spectacles for the day. Lulu of course needs them for her own schoolwork, but unfortunately an exam takes precedence over a day of ordinary lessons. Girls not speaking to each other, and Lulu is not speaking to me.

FRIDAY 14 NOVEMBER

My discipline is slipping. Lulu had detention after school tonight – for uniform and jewellery issues. We picked her up from school at 4.15pm and dropped her at the movies for long-standing evening with friends. I gave her $20.00 to go with. And she relieved me of my shoes, handbag and make-up before getting out of the truck! Really must be more masterful. Will begin shortly.

SATURDAY 15 NOVEMBER

Today was the husband's 50th birthday. Long-planned trip into Sydney for dinner at Circular Quay was abandoned in favour of emergency trip into Narellan to buy new glasses for Annie. Parted with another $400.00 for another pair of Dolce and Gabbana glasses, exactly the same as Lulu's.

Girls busy with friends tonight, so the husband and I celebrated his birthday at an Italian restaurant in Camden. It certainly wasn't Sydney Harbour, but we had a romantic evening.

SUNDAY 16 NOVEMBER

Husband and I went for coastal drive and pulled-up at a little harbour used by small private fishing boats. Was very excited to see six or seven HUGE pelicans lined up on the rocks. I walked right up to them and they didn't move away. I leant against a stone picnic table, and the birds all turned to stare at me and then started shuffling closer – Jasper Conran was terrified, and I was a bit perturbed. I suddenly realised that the 'picnic' table was actually a 'fish-gutting' table, where the fishermen gut their catch and throw the heads to the pelicans!

PART THREE
The Chicken Man's House

WEEK 46
Persona Non Grata in Prada

MONDAY 17 NOVEMBER

A problem has arisen. The husband called at the Chicken Shop tonight, to introduce himself to Toni and purchase BBQ chicken for dinner. Toni was very amiable, and the husband expressed his gratitude at Toni's kindness re the rental house. All was going well until Toni dropped the bombshell that Jasper Conran must NOT, under any circumstances, be allowed in the house. Toni pointed out that there is a shed in the garden where he will expect JC to live and sleep. Dare not tell Jasper.

TUESDAY 18 NOVEMBER

Feeling very upset. Why do the Australians appear to be uptight about dogs being inside? Most dogs here are decreed to be 'outside dogs,' probably due to the warm weather, I expect. We are moving house tomorrow and once again will have to go through the charade of Jasper Conran officially living outside.

WEDNESDAY 19 NOVEMBER

Moving day went very well, thankfully. The husband had arranged for a removal company to do the job this time, and our meagre possessions were removed from the Doll's House and deposited at the Chicken Man's House in under two hours. Girls returned home from school to find they are now back in possession of a huge bedroom each, complete with a long wall of fitted-wardrobes and built-in mirrors. They are overjoyed.

Jasper Conran is not so overjoyed. The new garden is very safely enclosed and we have taken the decision to make him stay outside during the day. The rear garden is enclosed by tall metal gates at each side of the house, and beyond this on the left-hand side is a very chic paved courtyard leading to the rear garage door. His kennel has been placed very carefully in the shade, and we bought him a new football and squeaky toys. It is doggy utopia.

THURSDAY 20 NOVEMBER

The rental agent will not be bothering us again until the 3-month inspection in February, and luckily it does not appear as if Toni will ever be making any unexpected trips to check up on illegal house-dogs. This is such a relief. I don't want to think about Jasper Conran 'spinning with the chickens' on Toni's rotisserie if he gets caught out!

FRIDAY 21 NOVEMBER

Busy day, unpacking kitchen and bathroom belongings. Takeaway pizza from Dominos tonight, as avoiding Toni from now on. Jasper and I will take a different route on our daily walk, so as not to remind the Italian gentleman of his existence.

SATURDAY 22 NOVEMBER

Trip into the city today, as Lulu needed to go to the Museum of Contemporary Arts to view something for her Visual Arts assignment.

After the museum, we went to view the exclusive shops. We window-shopped at Gucci, Chanel and Louis Vuitton, but then Lulu dragged me actually IN to Prada to look at a bracelet she is coveting. The doorman was very polite, but he appeared to pointedly look down at my feet – I am probably the only person in the world to enter a Prada shop wearing Apple Pie trainers! My stylish new persona has let me down. Must buy new shoes as soon as possible.

SUNDAY 23 NOVEMBER

The husband has set up a direct debit to pay the rent. This will alleviate the necessity of me having to trail into Narellan every Monday morning. I pretended to be relieved, but had actually been counting on a regular gallivanting trip. The husband seems to be becoming wise to my schemes. Have been cut-off at source.

WEEK 47
Chanel Jackets & Ray-Bans
(Both Fake!)

MONDAY 24 NOVEMBER

Finally, I'm back where I belong – living in a huge house with en-suite bathroom has once again lifted my spirits. This house is turning me back into a Chanel jacket and designer jeans kind of girl. The other house turned me into a baggy old jogging bottoms and washed-out t-shirt kind of tired old hag. Sadly, my jacket is not Chanel, but a very nice Boden, and my jeans are not designer, but BigW. Life is definitely back on track, despite the BigW jeans.

TUESDAY 25 NOVEMBER

Woke up today feeling just so cheerful. Have decided to abandon worrying altogether and have mentally torn-up both my Worry Lists. (Think cheery demeanour was aided enormously by the discovery of a fabulous pair of fake Ray-Ban sunglasses for only $12.00!)

WEDNESDAY 26 NOVEMBER

Cockroaches are proving a bit of a problem. They appear to enter from the garage and dash along the corridor into the kitchen. I spray the garage door with Mortein every evening before bed, and when I get up the next morning the corridor has turned into Death Alley, with dead and dying cockroaches littered in relays along the tiled floor. In the last few days though, only two 'roaches have made it as far as the kitchen, so I think I'm winning.

THURSDAY 27 NOVEMBER

We're having a bit of a tussle with the previous rental agent. Husband rang them again today, and they have still not signed-off the house as being left in a satisfactory condition in order that we can reclaim our bond. I am not happy. The landlady has allegedly verbally told them she's happy, but they won't release the bond until she puts this in writing. Am particularly cross seeing as her house is 100% cleaner than when we moved in, we've left her two pristinely decorated bedrooms, mended the wonky shelves and put up a new blind in the gap where one was missing. If we haven't heard by Monday, I'm tempted to start quoting the Retail Tenancy Act to them.

FRIDAY 28 NOVEMBER

Day out at Macarthur Square. Husband chauffeured me there and back, as he was working in the area. Almost went to see Nicole's new film, 'Australia,' but couldn't face sitting down for three hours. Might go next week. Went shopping instead. Bought some cute Christmas cards to send back home. Have decided not to send presents this year, and hope people understand. We're still struggling with rent and mortgage payments (but am no longer worrying about it) and cannot afford to buy presents and pay for extortionate postage.

SATURDAY 29 NOVEMBER

Living a more glamorous life in the new house has made me realise once again that I'm still not getting out enough to the right sort of places, so with this in mind, husband, Jasper and I went to Mosman this afternoon. Mosman is a chic, millionaire enclave north of the harbour.

As we drove over the harbour bridge the sun was shining on my Ray-Bans (!), there was a massive cruise liner in Darling Harbour, and luxury yachts and motor boats were sailing up and down beneath us. We drove to Mosman and parked up to walk around and browse the (very expensive) exclusive shops. Pedigree dogs and designer handbags were out in abundance and Jasper Conran was admired many times, despite me only carrying an Elizabeth Hurley beach bag which was free in last month's Instyle magazine!

We bought gourmet sandwiches from The Cheese Shop and drove to Bradley's Head to eat them. From our parking spot we could view practically the whole of the harbour – if Nicole had been in her back garden, we could have waved to each other! Private helicopters were buzzing above our heads, and aqua planes were zooming around and landing with a splash almost in front of us! Must keep up with this life and not slip back into being content with trundling around in the backwaters.

<u>SUNDAY 30 NOVEMBER</u>

Lulu went out to a pool party yesterday, to celebrate her friend's birthday. She and Hilary spent ages getting ready, only for the boys to throw them in the pool as soon as they arrived! If looks could kill, I'm sure those boys would be six foot under!

WEEK 48
Cool Hand Jasper

MONDAY 1 DECEMBER

The husband is away in Parramatta tonight, with his boss. When they returned to their hotel after their meal out, they discovered there was a power cut and the whole place was in darkness. Instead of retiring to bed like normal people, they headed to the bar anyway and drank gallons of beer by torchlight!

TUESDAY 2 DECEMBER

Jasper Conran is in disgrace. He has been tunnelling his way out of the back garden. He was discovered in the side courtyard, barking at the rear garage door, covered in dirt from nose to tail. When we refused to answer the door, he tunnelled under the gate again and went back to his kennel.

WEDNESDAY 3 DECEMBER

Before the husband went to work today, he barricaded the garden gate with a plank of wood and the heavy wooden airline crate in which Jasper travelled to Australia. It took Mr Conran approximately 3 minutes to push the crate out of the way, remove the plank of wood and tunnel under the gate.

THURSDAY 4 DECEMBER

Yesterday was my sister's 20th wedding anniversary, and when I spoke to her this evening she was very upset because she hadn't received so much as a card from her chief bridesmaid. I was appalled. I mean, how much effort does it take to buy a card and a stamp and put them in the post box? It's just disgraceful. I hope she will soon forgive me.

FRIDAY 5 DECEMBER

I have been to see a chiropractor today, as back/leg/disc have been causing me agony yet again. Think it was the upheaval of the move and all the cleaning that must have upset it. Have been very worried because the pain is sometimes unbearable.

Anyway, chiropractor was really nice and feels sure she can help. She performed an 'adjustment,' which was not as scary as it sounded, and I felt better almost straight away! Am a bit worried though, about her pronouncement that my left leg is significantly shorter than my right! I hope it's just the pain and tension that has caused it to temporarily contract.

Had a stroll down to the outdoor pool in Camden and was very impressed. Luckily, the chiropractor wants to see me every week beginning January, so I made a mental plan that in future will attend appointment then purchase delicious smoked salmon sandwiches from the Gourmet Deli, a magazine from the newsagent and then spend the afternoon at the pool. Life is looking up. Must get back on diet immediately, as will need to purchase swimsuit.

SATURDAY 6 DECEMBER

Keeping up to the High Life takes some energy – thank goodness I only do it once a week. Went back to Double Bay today to spend some Christmas present money at the chic stationery shop. Had to send the husband off round the arcades by himself, as couldn't concentrate with him breathing down my neck and muttering at the prices.

Decided to buy a pen so chose three designs I liked, and the nice assistant took me to sit down and try them out. This was a bit more embarrassing than it sounds, because my handwriting is atrocious and definitely not worthy of the sleek pens. However, he politely didn't comment on my scruffy scribblings, but neatly gift-wrapped my chosen pen while I carried-on browsing. Just as he'd finished wrapping though, I spotted a display case which I'd missed the first time round, and changed my mind! (He was very gracious and un-wrapped the first one, then wrapped up the second with barely a sigh).

Couldn't decide what else to buy – until I spotted the packets of sealing wax and elegant little wax seals. From now on, all my correspondence will resemble the Magna Carta. Must work on the handwriting. Must also work on not setting the house on fire, as predicted by the husband.

Quick trip to the Chocolate Shop after shopping, for a cookies and cream sundae and a lemon granita. All the women in the Chocolate Shop were very elegant and also very thin – felt slightly uncomfortable (ie, a greedy pig) as I gobbled down my sundae while they sipped their skinny lattes!

Browsed the rental agent windows before we left, and spotted a lovely Double Bay house to rent – for only $10,500.00 per week!!! Drove home through various scenic bays, past the famous Doyle's fish restaurant, through Bondi and back to Narellan. Didn't mind coming home as do not possess the energy to be a jet-setter 7 days per week, and anyway, the high level of intensive groom-ing required to live at the coast would leave no time for anything else.

SUNDAY 7 DECEMBER

Mr Conran is very tenacious. He was discovered this morning with his head and shoulders through the cat-flat in the laundry room door. Husband barricaded the flap with a broken insect screen he found beside the garage, but JC managed to pull that out in about 20 minutes. We're taking bets on what he'll try next. Husband is thinking of buying him a mini-motorbike to see if he can clear the fence!

WEEK 49
A Mouse in the House

MONDAY 8 DECEMBER

Jasper Conran has turned orange from digging in the dry, dusty dirt.

TUESDAY 9 DECEMBER

Last day of peace and quiet for 8 weeks. Girls finished school at lunchtime, and don't return until the end of January. Husband took them to Speech Night this evening. I managed to escape as my damaged disc prevents me from sitting for long periods on hard chairs. Enjoyed a nice evening with Jasper Conran, watching dvds and drinking Diet Coke. Really must resume job search.

WEDNESDAY 10 DECEMBER

Scary, scary day. Annie was out with the boyfriend, and Lulu and I decided to unpack the boxes stacked in the study. We were down to the last box when we spotted a mouse! All hell broke loose. After we'd finished screaming and clutching each other in panic, Lulu jumped on a chair by the laptop and tried to book a flight home – she's been living on a knife-edge after finding a cockroach in her room yesterday, so a mouse was the final straw.

Eventually persuaded her down from the chair, and we laid a trap. We armed ourselves with a broom each, put some cheese down on the floor in front of us and sat still and silent on our chairs.

After a couple of minutes, the mouse peeked out from under the fridge and headed towards the cheese. It darted in and out a few times before it plucked-up enough courage to go right up to the cheese and start nibbling.

While it was stuffing its face, I threw my broom across the kitchen and sent the mouse skidding into the skirting board. Lulu was supposed to follow this up with a killer-blow from her broom before the mouse could recover. However, at the last moment she decided the poor little creature was too cute and she couldn't bring herself to kill it. Had to leave husband to lay a humane trap tonight and hope it takes the bait. Think it will, as it appeared to be a bit greedy.

THURSDAY 11 DECEMBER

Hallelujah – Bruce was in the trap when we got up this morning. Husband sealed it with duct tape and we released it a few miles up the road. Strictly speaking, the husband released it while Lulu and I watched from the truck, as it was absolutely POURING with rain and we didn't want to ruin our hairstyles. (The husband has very little hair and, indeed, no discernible style to ruin). Couldn't help thinking that the mouse would probably be back home before us, but we'll see.

After pest-releasing duties, the husband gave Lulu and I a lift to the Westfield shopping centre near the city. Had a brilliant day. Lulu had a wad of Christmas cash from Gran to spend. We checked out the Benefit make-up counter first but she was spoiled for choice, so we decided to take a brochure and read it while we had breakfast. We enjoyed warm banana bread and orange juice while she decided. Trouble is, though, when you read the Benefit brochure, you start to think that you need absolutely EVERYTHING in there and how can you POSSIBLY live without it? Headed back to the cosmetic counters and after an hour or so (yawn) she chose a Benefit gift box with four lovely products in it. We then trailed to David Jones to buy Marc Jacobs' Daisy perfume and Clinique lip glosses.

When she'd spent all her money we headed to the cinema and watched 'Four Christmases.' The husband collected us at 5.00pm and the journey home took around three hours due to volume of traffic and lack of suitable roads. The Sydney town planners should be locked-up.

SATURDAY 13 DECEMBER

I am such a fool. Have just realised that for the last few months I've been taking dead thyroid tablets. No wonder I can't lose weight, despite subsisting on nothing, and no wonder I've been falling asleep whenever I sit down for more than 3 minutes. I thought I had narcolepsy!

I've been so distracted by the pain in my back/leg that I didn't realise my tablets had expired. Also, the fridge had a blip a few months ago and froze everything within it, so that would have killed the thyroxine straight away. I don't like these Australian tablets. Have looked on the internet to see if I could buy my usual supply, and discovered you can do so very easily – but Australia will not allow them to be imported. Have been to GP's emergency surgery this morning for blood tests and new prescription.

WEEK 50
Another Mouse
in the House

MONDAY 15 DECEMBER

News via school is that girls have done very well in their recent exams, so husband and I decreed they were to be given $100.00 each to spend on a trip to Luna Park with their friends.

Collected new prescription today, and this brand is much better than the last one. These are in a blister pack instead of a bottle, and look very similar to my UK tablets.

TUESDAY 16 DECEMBER

Have been browsing the job market again – with no success. I rang practically all the employment agencies in this area again, and they almost laughed down the 'phone at me. Was told the only decent jobs are in the city. Cannot possibly travel to the city every day. Train service is not reliable, and the journey from here to the station is gridlocked every day. Would have to get up at 4.00am every day in order to get there, and would not be home until 7.00 or 8.00pm. How would Jasper Conran cope by himself all day? Who would cook dinner for my starving children upon their return home from school? There must be SOME way of earning extra money and alleviating my boredom.

WEDNESDAY 17 DECEMBER

Do not laugh. Am now an Avon lady! Saw advert on internet this morning, sent email immediately and Area Manager was knocking on my door at 1.00pm! Got ready for meeting with great care; nails varnished, immaculate make-up, hair straightened etc. as felt should project a poised and polished image in order to land the job. (Briefly wondered if should get hair shampooed and set, then remembered that Reese Witherspoon is new Avon spokeswoman and thus Avon is now cool). Anyway, needn't have bothered. It seems they give Avon territories to anyone who asks. Have been given approx. 70 houses near me to target as a bit of a trial. Manager explained that you need more than one territory to make a viable business, as opposed to just a hobby, but that I have to start off small and see how it goes. Unfortunately, she can't let me start until after Christmas. Must not be deterred. Will give it my best shot.

THURSDAY 18 DECEMBER

Was summoned by GP to attend urgent appointment this afternoon. Thyroid levels are totally out of kilter. Not surprising my diets don't work. It's a miracle I've had the energy to get out of bed these last few months. Have been given form to get another blood test taken in two months' time, to check that levels are back up and functioning normally. Hopefully, will now start to see results from all my dietary deprivation. (Ignored husband muttering about recent excesses in the Chocolate Shop).

FRIDAY 19 DECEMBER

Annie was invited to friend's house this evening, for a scary movie night. Husband dropped her off and came back awestruck – said it was the biggest house he'd ever seen, at the end of a private road, out in the countryside past Cobbitty. Well, of course I just had to go with him when he went to collect her, so I could see for myself.

This seemed like a good idea at the time, but within 5 mins I was scared stiff. We had to drive down the wildlife corridor in the pitch black darkness, and almost ran over a wombat. It was quite big, like a miniature bear. I was terrified a kangaroo would jump out on us. We arrived at the house and I made the husband get out to knock on the door, as I was too scared to leave the truck. He said I should sound the alarm if anything pounced and dragged him off into the bushes! Anyway, the door opened and he disappeared safely inside. For TEN minutes. While I had to sit ALONE in the truck surrounded by pitch-black nothingness. I was very relieved when door finally opened and he reappeared with Annie, Lauren and Hannah, but I was very cross that he'd had a tour of the mansion while I was shaking with fear outside!

SATURDAY 20 DECEMBER

Cannot believe it is Christmas next week. Have not bought any presents. Cannot really afford any presents. The gardens on Harrington Park are all decorated with fancy lighting, but it just seems ludicrous in this heat. Carols were playing in the shopping centre in Narellan today, while everyone walked around in shorts (not me, obviously). Only good thing about the lack of Christmas spirit in our house is that girls don't appear to expect too much in the way of gifts. Thank goodness they won't be disappointed then!

SUNDAY 21 DECEMBER

Husband has been setting the humane mousetrap every evening, just in case there was more than one of the little rodents, and to my dismay there was another one in there this morning. Didn't inform girls, just smuggled it out to truck for later release. Have instructed the husband to take it miles and miles away, preferably into another state altogether.

I've been very upset by the mice, but tonight the husband was chuckling about them. When I asked how he could possibly find it amusing, he said he'd just realised there was absolutely no chance of my sister coming to visit now, as she's very afraid of them. The husband is very cheeky. Gave him a severe telling-off.

WEEK 51
It'll Be Lonely This Christmas

MONDAY 22 DECEMBER

The teenagers are running rings around me. I spend all my time trying, and failing, to keep them in-line.

Sent Annie to the mall this morning to look for a new dress. We have been invited to a BBQ party on Boxing Day, with the husband's boss and his family, and although it will be very casual, I want her to get something new. Arranged to meet her in Borders at 1.00pm so I could go and pay for whatever she had chosen. She came strolling up, hand-in-hand with the boyfriend, and announced that she hadn't managed to look for anything yet. Drew some money out, gave her $80.00 and told her to go and find something. Just arrived home when I received a text from her announcing that she couldn't find anything suitable and was at the movies instead!

Lulu has been roaming around Harrington Park recently with three boys from school, and another boy who is the cousin of one of them. Late afternoon she asked if she could go to Sam's house, so I let her go and told her to be home for 8.00pm. Well, of course, 8.00pm came and went and still no sign of Lulu. By now it was almost dark, so I was getting worried. Rang her mobile a million times – no answer. Sent a million texts – no answer. Rang Sam's house – no answer. Was utterly furious, as had just changed into lounging shorts and replaced contact lenses with glasses in order to settle down for relaxing hour watching Bones. Instead, had to set off walking to Sam's house to try and find her. Got there, and knocked on door. Was slightly taken aback when door swung open to reveal Christmas party in full-swing. Lulu very sheepishly apologised for not answering phone, and asked if she could stay longer as she had a lift home. Was tempted to say no, but felt that having her mother turn up on the doorstep in shorts and glasses in front of her cool friends was punishment enough, so relented.

You might wonder why I had to walk all the way across Harrington Park in the dark, by myself. The answer is due to the fact that the husband is away living it up in Melbourne at the Polyplas Christmas party. While I chase around the Narellan countryside after our children, his only worry is whether he can make it to the airport for a 9.00am flight home after a night of heavy partying.

TUESDAY 23 DECEMBER

Husband arrived home in very fragile state. Made him go out shopping with me to buy presents for girls. He was too exhausted to protest at amount of money spent, and his blurry eyes were unable to focus on whatever the tills were ringing up, so had quite a spending spree. (Still nothing compared to what would have been spent at home, of course. This will be our first married Christmas in which we haven't been overdrawn by 1st January!)

WEDNESDAY 24 DECEMBER

This is just so weird. We can't possibly celebrate Christmas in this heat. Went food shopping with husband and bought lots of treats. Will diet after Xmas. Is very strange to think that we won't see any of our family and friends over next few days. Think Skype will be doing overtime this week.

Lounged around from late afternoon onwards, sitting out on patio, sipping wine, reading, watching tv. All feels very strange. Would normally be on a knife-edge, running around doing last-minute errands, cleaning house, wrapping presents, delivering cards, baking mince pies and getting tipsy in pub with friends. Makes a nice change to have a break from all the chaos.

THURSDAY 25 DECEMBER

Had a great day. Left stockings on girls' beds and they woke up around 9.00am and brought them into our room. Lulu received an ipod Nano, and Annie a digital camera. Both also opened books, chocolates and perfume. Luckily, they had quite a lot of parcels from home to open, so they also received diamante key rings, pyjamas, jewellery, socks, purses and t-shirts. Jasper Conran was very pleased with his edible Christmas card!

Set off to Cronulla, and was amazed at amount of traffic on roads. It seems the whole of Australia goes to the beach on Christmas day. They were all having picnics and BBQs on the sand and in the parks. We bought fish and chips for lunch and drove along the coastline for a few miles. Weather was absolutely BOILING, and far too hot to stay out for long. Got home about 5.00pm and made a roast turkey dinner. Ended the evening by watching National Lampoon's Christmas Vacation! Husband was happy as a sandboy.

FRIDAY 26 DECEMBER

While we're away at the party in Bundanoon, Jasper has been booked-in with a company called "Don't Fret Pet," and he's staying with an old lady called Nancy who lives a few miles away from us. He cried when we left him, but I'm sure he'll be ok. I told her he was allowed a few treats, so I expect he'll soon cheer up. When she showed us around the garden, she pointed out her husband who's buried under the flowerbed (I presume she means his ashes). I just hope Mr Conran doesn't decide to dig him up.

The drive to Bundanoon was lovely. You could almost think you were in Norfolk, with the green fields and high hedgerows. The husband's boss met us at the Bundanoon Country Motel to check-in, and then took us to meet the family. They were all so kind and welcoming to us. We met his mum and dad again, his sister and brother with their families, and his wife and their three little boys. We had a great time. Bundanoon is very near to Kangaroo Valley, and on the map it appears to be right on the edge of the forest. When we were sitting in the garden, someone remarked that if we walked 300 metres behind us, we'd come to a sheer drop down the valley! Didn't bother to check it out.

The weather was so hot all day, and we sat in the front garden drinking champagne and enjoying a BBQ meal on long trestle tables which stretched the length of the lawn. In the evening we ate toasted ham and cheese sandwiches and glasses of wine before we left for the motel. It was the most exotic Boxing Day we've ever had, as there were kookaburras and parrots in the tree above our heads, when we're used to rain and ice and a glimpse of a robin if we're lucky!

We left our kind hosts around 9.30pm and went back to the motel. We were all tucked up in our beds and watching Miss Marple by 10.00pm. We were in a Family Room, so our beds were all in a row. The naughty husband scared us all silly by saying there was a mad axeman in the bathroom. It was pitch-black outside and as I was nearest the bathroom door, I made him swap beds!

SATURDAY 27 DECEMBER

Left the motel by 8.30am and drove to Berrima. Ate breakfast at a gourmet café (almond croissant and orange juice – have decided that diet can wait until next year) and just had time to pop into the stationery/bookbinding shop next door. Bought some cute ladybird notelets to send thank-you notes for Christmas presents.

Collected Jasper from Nancy at 10.30am – you should have heard him cry when he saw me! Thank goodness he hasn't dug-up the flowerbed. It sounded as if he led Nancy a bit of a merry dance last night though. He got in bed with her, but decided it was too warm so wandered around the bungalow until he decided to settle down. I hope she doesn't fill in the questionnaire with "No" to the question, "Would you look after this dog again?"

Had a very lazy day as we're all exhausted after being out in the sun all day yesterday. Jasper and I had a nap in the late afternoon. Had planned to go out for dinner, but no-one could be bothered to get ready so we snacked on turkey sandwiches instead.

WEEK 52
Sparkly Fireworks and Sexy Cowboys

MONDAY 29 DECEMBER

The family have been driving me mad – the teenagers are stroppy, the husband is grumpy and the dog is clingy – so I escaped this morning and caught the bus to Macarthur Square. Had Caesar salad for lunch, then went to the movies to watch, 'The Curious Case of Benjamin Button.' Found the film very strange, almost disturbing, and also very long – one minute longer than 'Australia.' Had a minor spending spree in the sales – bought a new purse, a book and some make-up. Arrived home around 7.00pm to find them all in slightly better mood, thank goodness.

TUESDAY 30 DECEMBER

Family are obviously keen to atone for their bad behaviour yesterday, as they all asked if I wanted to go to the coast for the afternoon. Decided to go to Wollongong, and had a lovely time – teenagers polite, husband smiling and even the dog didn't whinge too much.

WEDNESDAY 31 DECEMBER

Spent New Year's Eve alone with Jasper Conran. Husband decided to take girls into Sydney to view the legendary firework display at the harbour. I didn't go for two reasons: 1) am severely claustrophobic and warnings were given on tv that record crowds were expected, and 2) couldn't leave Jasper alone with fireworks blasting away all night.

Had a great time though, watching fireworks on tv with bottle of wine and box of chocs beside me. Family kept ringing me to relay events from the harbourside. They watched the 9.00pm family firework display and then decided to stay until the midnight one too. They finally arrived home around 4.00am. They had a great time, but apparently I had the best view and the most comfortable seat!

THURSDAY 1 JANUARY

Family were exhausted and slept all morning, but managed to rally in time for a video link with sister's family at midnight in UK. Was very strange to watch them doing their Irish jigs without us, but luckily the husband managed to work up enough energy to perform a little jig in his shorts. You could hear the laughter all the way from Lancashire to Sydney!

FRIDAY 2 JANUARY

Annie has been reunited with the boyfriend after his vacation in Kangaroo Valley, so the husband and I decided to go to Bowral for the afternoon. Felt a bit guilty, as I went in all the shops and husband had to wait outside with JC, as usual. Jasper was very naughty and barked at everyone for attention, so when we got home I put him outside in his kennel so he could reflect upon his bad behaviour.

SATURDAY 3 JANUARY

Oh my goodness. Have been to a rodeo. It was SO exciting. Couldn't get near the ring when we first arrived, so went around the back where the contestants were, and mingled with the cowboys! You should have seen them. There they were in their stetsons with their leather chaps strapped around their slim hips, and their cowboy boots and silver spurs. And there was my husband. In his shorts and sandals. And there were the cowgirls in their tight jeans and checked shirts. And there was me in my BigW jeans and my Target t-shirt!

We watched the barrel-racing and then walked to the pub for a drink, but we arrived back just in time for the bull-riding. It was SO scary. I was leaning against a yellow metal fence waiting for it to start, when the husband came up and stated that the bull was right behind me! I jumped out of my skin and when I looked round the corner, the bull was indeed right behind me, fastened in a tight pen while the cowboy fastened the rope around him. We were separated only by a few millimetres of metal.

It was all very scary when the gate opened and the bull charged out. The first cowboy stayed on for almost 9 seconds, but all the others were off in less than 2. One bull, called Maniac, went absolutely berserk and all the rodeo staff had to jump up onto the fence to get away from him. I stated that I wouldn't get on a bull for any amount of money in the world, but the husband said that he'd do it for $100,000.00. It was announced over the tannoy that the cowboys receive $1,000.00 per attempt and the prize money was $15,000.00, so they obviously couldn't afford to put my husband in the ring. (Actually, I think I upset him a bit when I said that the bull might not be able to buck him off because he probably weighed the equivalent of three cowboys)!

SUNDAY 4 JANUARY

Went for a quick walk with Jasper Conran this afternoon, and returned to find the husband holding an inquest into the origins of some pink powdery substance he'd found on the kitchen counter. He was more or less accusing the teenagers of handling drugs, but calmed down when I explained it was actually the residue of two pink meringues I bought the girls this morning. Think the sun is addling his brain.

WEEK 53
A Whole Year in Sydney

MONDAY 5 JANUARY

The Avon Manager came to see me this afternoon. She explained my brochures will be delivered at the end of the week, and gave me a map of my 'territory.' Cannot wait to earn some extra money.

TUESDAY 6 JANUARY

I am melting. Today has apparently been the hottest Sydney day on record for four years. The car temperature gauge said 44 degrees this afternoon, it was awful. Mr Conran and I spent the afternoon lying on my bed with the air-conditioning on full-blast, alternately reading and snoozing.

WEDNESDAY 7 JANUARY

If it doesn't cool down soon, I will have to go back home. Newspaper announced today that there is a record number of deadly funnel-web spiders on the loose, as the hot weather is bringing them out in droves. It advises people to shake out their shoes before putting them on, as the creepy-crawlies are sometimes found indoors. Doubt I will sleep tonight. Might pack suitcase instead.

THURSDAY 8 JANUARY

Been to huge shopping mall this afternoon with husband and daughter. Was supposed to be only window-shopping, but somehow ended-up buying Lulu some Benefit Eyecon cream, a cd, two new tops and a pair of denim leggings! How on earth did that happen? Made the fatal mistake of sending the husband off to read his paper over a cup of coffee, leaving shopaholic daughter and I free to make illegal purchases.

FRIDAY 9 JANUARY

Have booked table at El Gusto's for dinner tomorrow night, to celebrate the anniversary of arriving in Sydney. Weather cool today. No spiders in sight. Have unpacked suitcase. Have decided to stay, although still far too fat for sunhat and swimsuit. Must implement very strict diet and exercise routine now that thyroid issues have been resolved. Will begin tomorrow.

Printed in Great Britain
by Amazon

49647335R00139